THE COWGIRL GETS THE BAD GUY

COWGIRL MYSTERIES, BOOK 1

SUSAN LOWER

Giddy Up!

THE COWGIRL GETS THE BAD GUY

1

There is nothing a girl looks forward to more than putting on her Sunday best and heading to town after a long winter in Deadwood's gulch. Except I haven't worn a dress in years, and the good ladies of the town have no problem stopping to stare as I walk into the mercantile with my list.

There is no shame in a hard day's work, and if these town ladies knew the things I did out at our claim, they'd never survive to break a sweat. Well, maybe Ruby, who runs the boarding house. She's a widow and I've already checked in with her for a room tonight. It's been too long since I caught up with my best friend, Ella Mae. I could kill Earl, my father, for insisting we could last a few more days. And that was until he traded his last bottle of firewater to Chief Tail Feathers. Gambled it, more likely, but our indigenous neighbors see no value in the bits of silver and gold we mine from the mountain. Tobacco, rifles, and firewater are more valuable than women, and that is saying something.

Old Man Jensen clears his throat and I slap my list down on his counter. His eyes are on the side of my face instead of on my list. I tuck a long curl of hair behind my ear that's slipped out of my hat, which tips it and lets the whole mess of waves fall down my back.

I sigh, knowing it came loose on the ride into town. I reach up to fix it as I hear the bell and someone calling my name.

"Jo! Jo!"

Jensen grabs the list, and I turn. Robbie, an errand boy in town, comes running up to me. "There you are," he huffs, trying to catch his breath. "You'd better come quick."

I haven't been in town for more than a few hours. Nobody knows I am here, and what could be so important for Robbie to come to fetch me?

I spot Lottie Larson and Hannah Baker with their baskets hanging off their arms and leaning a little too close to one another. They're whispering, and I have a feeling it has more to do with Robbie coming in after me than the fact I'm wearing pants.

"What? Where?" I'm trying to process what I should do.

"Earl is in the saloon and gone and tossed you in the pot."

I blink, taking a second to comprehend what this young boy is saying.

Jensen pulls the list away from the counter. "You'd best go see what this is about, Jo. I'll take care of this and have it ready for when you get back."

There's a cramping in my belly, and it isn't from lack of food. I take a glance at Hannah and Lottie and that feeling twists deeper. Lottie lifts an eyebrow and I avoid her gaze. *Dear Lord in heaven,* I pray silently, *please don't let it be so.*

I turn on my bootheel and hightail it out of there as quick as I can. I all but run down the wooden sidewalk to get to the local watering hole.

Robbie runs ahead, stopping me before I push through the swinging saloon doors. "On second thought, you shouldn't go in there."

I plant my hands on my hips. "And why not?"

He's a cute kid with hazel eyes and dark brown hair that splits at the side because of a cowlick. Poor kid is stuck in that in-between age—he's not old enough to be treated like man, but still young enough he's got that softness to his face. Everyone knows Robbie is Amaryllis's son, even if no one knows who his father is. I'm not even sure Amaryllis does, but it's not for me to judge on what she does for a living or who she does it with.

I shudder a little and reach to grab hold of those swinging doors when Amaryllis shoves them open for me. She's wearing a deep red skirt with a black corset. It's late in the afternoon and, judging by the paint on her face, she has been hanging out in this hot box for a while.

"Good job, Robbie." She pats the boy on the head. "Now you get before there is trouble." She hands him a coin, and he takes off.

She ushers me through the saloon. There are a few men at the bar. One tips his hat at me, and I avert my eyes. It's early yet, and I wager it won't be long before the ranch hands and the Friday night crowd show up.

Amaryllis has a feather in the back of her hair with lace and ribbon. She's tied up her curls and left her neck bare. Although her appearance is daring, it doesn't attract as much attention as I do.

There's something about a girl in pants men seem to drop their jaw over. I am about to tell Amaryllis she should switch to pants when I spot the table in the far back. My gut burns clear up my throat as I march over to Earl.

He's sitting with three other men and, sure enough, I see the written note on top of the cash and coin on the table. I don't even bother checking out his hand. Two of the players I recognize. It's Jed Warner from the hotel and Buck Dawson from out at the Triple D Ranch. The fourth guy is a stranger. He glances up at me, not at all shy to check me out from head to toe. It turns that twist in my stomach into something down-right unladylike. Dressed in a fancy suit with dark lapels, this man has got a silver striped vest beneath and a watch chain in his vest pocket. I'd almost think he was a banker, but Campbell Reed runs the bank in Deadwood. No, this man is too clean cut. He's not wearing a hat, and there isn't one hanging on his chair either. He's holding a hand of cards at ease, and I watch as he tugs at his sleeve.

I catch the emerald glint of his eyes, and Amaryllis moves closer to him. Taking a step behind Earl, I notice he's not got any coin left, and my breath hitches. Curling and uncurling my hands, I stare down at him.

"Don't you gooo looking at meeee like that, girl," Earl slurs and waves his hand. "I *told* youuu I had a daughter, didn't I?"

The stranger tilts back, his eyes doing a slow sweep of me. "You call that a girl?"

My jaw falls a little. I glance down at my chest, and yep, a man would have to be blind not to notice these sisters. I cross my arms, hefting them up a little, then let my arms fall away. *What in the world am I doing?*

I glower as Amaryllis slides an arm around the stranger's shoulder, leans down, and gives her head a slight tilt as if she's trying to tell me something.

"Why don't you buy me a drink after this round?"

Buck is chewing on a toothpick and gaffs at the stranger's remark. "I can see why he keeps her locked away in that mine of his."

A lock of hair falls across my eye. Pushing it back, I fix my hat to keep the stray contained.

"I'm out," Jed tosses in his cards. "I got nothing."

"You got something other than that girl of yours?" Buck taps his cards, his eyes on Earl.

"Just my mine." Earl clutches his cards, and my lungs tighten as I spy his hand. He's put our claim and me on those cards. There is no way anyone is going to beat his hand unless they've got an ace up their sleeve.

"Then I'd say it's time to show those hands, gentleman," the stranger declares.

"Wait one minute" I step between my father and Buck. "Don't you got to raise the stakes or something?" My heart is beating fast. "Please tell me you didn't bet our mine on a card game!"

"Oh no, darlin'." The stranger grinned. "He went and bet you first."

I gasp and glare down at Earl. "You *what?*"

"At least the mine is worth something." Earl reaches out and shoves me aside. "Now mind your business."

My father has one thing right. The mine is worth something, *a whole lot* of somethings, or should I say someones? There is no way I'm going to remind him here in front of these folks exactly what our claim is worth and why it's so important we keep a hold of it.

Looking down at the pile of coins and cash, I can't help thinking Earl has put every red cent we have on this game. I should have known better than to leave the old man to his own devices. I growl, frustrated, and Buck glances up at me. Amaryllis sucks in her breath and the world feels a little shaky.

Mr. Fancy Pants shows his cards. Earl drops his hand. The ace is out of the hole, and Mr. Fancy Pants has the better hand. Earl jumps to his feet, his face turning beet red and fuming. Frozen with shock, I watch as the stranger pulls the pile of cash and coin toward him.

Buck grabs his hand. "Hold up there."

Earl reaches for his gun, but he left his rifle hidden on our wagon.

Buck tosses his cards, leans in, and stares at the stranger. "How long you been holding that ace?"

Amaryllis's eyes widen. Maybe what I took for a signal to

me had been for Buck. Jed's gone from the table. He's leaning over by the bar and grabbing a drink.

"Apparently long enough," says the stranger, scooping up his winnings. Before he can snatch the IOU made out by Earl, I reach for it. The stranger is quicker. He plucks it right from under my hand. He winks at me and nods at Earl. "It's been a pleasure playing with you gentlemen."

"You're a cheat," Earl bellows.

The stranger pales for a moment. Swiftly, he gathers up his cash and tucks it in his pocket. He folds the promissory note, a.k.a IOU entitling him to my father's mine and me. Smugly, the fancy pants gambler pats it in his pocket. "Is that any way to speak to your future son-in-law?"

"Pfft," I blow at him. "I'm not marrying you."

Buck stands, stretches his arms, and motions for Amaryllis to join him. "Good luck with that one."

"Wait. You're gonna walk away?"

Buck shrugs, puts his arm around Amaryllis, and heads for the bar. She tilts her chin up, looking down at Earl, and makes a sound in her throat. You'd think she was the one whose hand in marriage he gambled away.

But Earl is shaking, his pointing finger wavering. "You take the girl, but the land is mine. You cheat!"

Mr. Fancy Pants Gambler keeps his hand over his money pocket. For a moment, he might even look a little sympathetic to our plight. Pitying himself, more likely. In the shadows of the saloon, I can tell he's not from around here. There isn't a callous on those hands or a stench of sweat coming from his body. I can smell lavender, and it makes me think this gambler has been bathing over at the Swanson Sisters' place. For a dollar, a man can get a bath and then some.

"I think I'll take them both," he says, holding out his hand to me. "Pierce Weston. I believe my future bride should at least know my name before we wed."

The gall of this man. Tight-lipped, I take his hand, only to find him slapping a few paper bills in my hand. "You take that and buy yourself a dress now. Something pretty and maybe a new bonnet, too. I'll meet you at the church." He looks around, and I feel my face turning hot.

Earl goes to snatch the cash from my hand, and I close my fingers around it. "What are you doing?" If I were any other female, I'd cry. My voice raises, and a group of cowboys having sauntered in from off the range glance my way.

"Give me the cash, girl. I'm getting my money back," Earl demands.

"Oh, no you don't." I walk right up and put my finger in the old man's chest. Behind me, I hear the gambler call for Robbie and tell him to fetch the preacher. "I'll see you at the church," he says and heads out of sight.

"You give meee that money, girl!" Earl demands.

It's the drink talking. Whenever my father is deep into the firewater, his words slur, and his brain slows.

"Have you any idea what you've done?" I hiss at him.

"Got rid of you." He snorts and reaches again for the cash in my hand.

"You lost our claim. What about Tail Feathers and the rest of them up on Standing Rock?" I keep my voice low for Earl's ears only.

And that's when it hits him. My father pales. Instantly, he ages by a decade. Then he wobbles like a woman about to pass out. He clutches onto me and the years flash in his gaze. He sags, and my heart softens to the spot where it aches for my old man. It's the firewater. It does it to him every time. He's mean and ornery as they come when he's drinking that stuff. It robs him of his sanity, and I can see the chill of sobriety coming through.

"You give me that money, Jo. Nobody cheats Earl Dean."

He proclaims it so loud even the dust-busting cowboys lining up at the bar take a moment to glance our way again.

Grabbing my hand, Earl tries to take the money when Amaryllis steps between us. "Heard Robbie took off for the preacher. I'd get down to Grace's place before she closes for the night. If she doesn't have something of your size, I can pull out something of mine. We can probably hold him off until morning seeing for the arrangements and all."

"You saw him, didn't youuu?" Earl turns, still flushed, toward Amaryllis. "He cheated. You watched it happen. You saw his hand."

"And there was an ace in it," Amaryllis says. Her eyes zero in on Earl. She motions for me to go as she attempts to console my father.

He's having nothing of it. "I'm going to the sheriff."

Jed slaps his hand down on my father's shoulder. "Sure you are, Earl. We all lost tonight. Let me buy you a drink."

"He'll geeet away. We can't let him geeet away!" My father storms out of the saloon, stumbling over his feet and leaving Amaryllis with her hands planted on her hips.

Buck comes up beside me, holding out a drink. "You might need this."

Some help he is. I'll need more than whiskey to clean up this mess.

I look down at the paper bills in my hand. It's not quite enough to cover the list of supplies at the mercantile. Tail Feathers won't be happy not to get his portion of tobacco my father promised him.

I can't help feeling as if a war is about to break loose.

It's probably better if I keep my pants on for when it does.

2

One must be prepared if they are to go to war.

I've got no one to blame but myself. I should have known better than to leave my father to his own devices. In the past, Earl would have headed to the claims office, got his money, and then gone to the bathhouse run by Emma and Eve Swanson. The twins had migrated their Southern charms to the west and made a fortune from it.

I twist my sisters to squish them back down after wrapping them in place beneath my camisole. I need more than a dress to show up at the church, and the cash in my hand won't cover a pair of drawers, let alone all the other frilly things to go along with it.

Nope, if the gambler catches up to me, he'll have to accept me for who I am, and I hope it is enough to change his mind.

Instead of going to Grace's for a dress, I went to see Mr. Jensen and pay for most of the list of goods I requested. *All I need to do is get the supplies loaded, find my father, and hightail it out of town before the gambler finds me.*

Part of me will miss seeing my best friend Ella Mae, but later I'll explain, and she'll understand. Her father is the preacher in Deadwood, and I know the good reverend well enough to know without just cause, he wouldn't force me to marry the gambler.

All I need to do is get back to our claim and make sure our stake is secure. This isn't the first time I'd left a man standing at the altar. My father had been at fault then, too. Eventually, I'll forgive him.

But Tail Feathers and those in his tribe are depending on us to bring back these supplies wouldn't be as forgiving. No tobacco, no keeping the chief and his tribe from crossing the reservation borders and raiding our place.

If not for Stands With Two Deer, I would have taken off a long time ago.

I spend the night hiding from the gambler. I'm sure Earl has retreated to a place no decent woman would dare go. Lucky for me, Ruby lets me in when she finds me at the back door. She even promises not to let anyone know I'm there. For all the gambler knows, I could be staying at the hotel.

In the morning, I finish braiding my hair, look at myself in the mirror, and catch the sun peeking through the window at Ruby's boarding house. It's time to get the show on the road.

The first place I go to is the stables to get my wagon and ponies. Hank, the blacksmith, stirs up the fire of his forge. It's barely the crack of dawn and the man has his shirt off. His big muscles flex as he breathes air into the forge to get the flames going. It's enough to make me hot and need to fan myself as I enter. The man is a sight to behold, and his wife is one lucky woman.

It doesn't take long to gather the ponies and wagon to park out in front of the mercantile. Thank goodness Hank demanded payment yesterday when my father and I dropped the ponies off. They're big, sturdy animals for climbing in the mountains. They might appear like cows from a distance, with their paint pattern of brown and white, if not for their thick necks and long manes.

"Them Indian ponies," Hank had asked when we first pull in with them. "You steal those off the reservation?"

"Trapper from the other side of the mountain." The answer my father gave satisfied Hank's curiosity. Lots of people come to the gulch around Deadwood. Not too many stay long before they move on. Everyone heads to California for the gold. No one ever has the patience to wait out for the motherlode.

I suppose we're the dumb ones.

Jensen isn't open for another hour. Knowing Earl, he's probably hung over somewhere around the saloon or the Swanson sisters' place. I'm going to have to go searching for him. He never came back to the boarding house. Ruby rented out his room for the night when it got late, and she had a last-minute inquiry. She was kind enough to give me credit for another night's stay for another time.

After checking the usual places, I head to the sheriff's office. Where else would a drunk go for the night to sleep it off?

The sky turns a dusty pink, with a glare of gold washing across the rooftops of the town. People are coming out on the sidewalks, and I can smell the scent of grease and fried chicken at the diner.

Grateful I've had my coffee, I hurry past the hotel and keep an eye out for my father and the gambler. I hope I run into the latter first but run straight into a solid body since I'm not look-ing. I hear an 'umph' and two hands reach out to grab me, preventing me from landing on my backside across the street from the hotel.

I have collided with the stormiest eyes I've ever seen. *Oh, me, oh my, this man is handsome.* His hat must have flown off as I ran into him, and it lies at my feet. He's got long, shoulder-length dark brown hair. His jaw is rough and shy of a few days' shave. I'm tempted to reach up and run my finger along the stubble.

"Watch where you're going."

"Well, that's rude," I say it out loud and cringe. One of these days I'll learn to put a filter on my mouth. Ella Mae says people who are alone most of the time don't know how to mind their manners as much. I don't need manners to see this guy is trouble with a capital T.

Taking a step back, I reach down to get his hat for him. As I snap back up, my head hits his chin and sends him staggering.

My hat flies back, and thankfully the cords keeping it dangling at my neck. I rub my head and squint at him. Holding out the hat, I squeak, "Sorry."

"You're a woman."

"You're a man." I straighten a little more, and the guy's chest puffs out. He's wearing a long duster, and underneath I can't help noticing he's packing some heat. My face turns hot as he snatches his hat from me and I almost trip again. I reach out and he stops me before I get a hold of something below the belt. And what a big holster that is.

I can almost feel the big guy upstairs frowning down on me. Where is Ella Mae with her Bible to thump me over the head when I need it?

Gah! I clutch my arms around me as he plunks that hat dangerously low on his head. "You looking for the sheriff?" he asks.

It takes a moment for his question to register through my mind. "The sheriff?"

"You're standing in front of the sheriff's office." He pulls back the side of his duster and plants a hand on the handle of a gun. More from habit, I surmise, than a threat, but dang, the man could make a girl swoon this early in the morning if not for having her coffee first.

Where's a lace fan when you need one?

I lick my lips and feign stupidity. Somehow, though, I'm not sure if it works on a guy like him. Those penetrating gray eyes darken and a riot breaks out inside my chest.

"Oh, no." I shake my head. "I'm not looking for the sheriff. I mean. I am. Maybe." I take a deep breath and try again. "What I mean is I'm looking for my father. I think the sheriff might have him locked up."

What every girl wants to admit when she first meets a man. I suppose I'll have to listen more to when Ella Mae tries to grace me with advice on relationships. One day, she'll make some man a good wife.

I can only hope someday I will, too, but if history is any sign, I fear I'll be just like my mother.

The man stands between me and the door.

"If you'll excuse me, I'd like to see the sheriff," I say.

"There's no one in there."

I try to look through the windows. "How do you know?"

He pulls out a cigar and lights it. I cough and wave away the smoke. "It's kind of early for that, isn't it?"

He puffs, creating a big plume of smoke, and grins. "He's down behind the saloon. Someone found a body."

Behind the saloon. A body.

"And you know this because?" I ask.

He clamps down on his cigar for a moment. Once he pulls it free of his mouth, he says, "I'm waiting for him to get back and pay my bounty." He points to the horses tied to the post in front of him. On the back of one is a bundle hanging over the saddle. I shudder, taking a step back. I'm pretty sure that's no sack of supplies, and with the man announcing there's another body down by the saloon, I pivot and run.

About to turn the corner between the saloon and the barbershop, a hand reaches out and grabs my shoulder.

"Hey there. I didn't mean to scare you."

I'm trembling and can't stop. I don't know why, but all I can think of is my father. I turn again to run to the back of the saloon.

Sheriff Bentely looks at me and steps away from the body. All I can see are a pair of tattered pants and a boot with a worn toe so thin it could fall apart at any moment.

I know before he even says a word. I know before those empathic eyes round on me. I know, because I've been telling my father he needs a new pair of boots for weeks and he promised we'd have enough money for all our needs this trip into town.

My heart skips a beat and another. My hands slap over my mouth, but the scream escapes before I can stop it. A pair of muscular arms gather around me and force me to turn away. The smell of tobacco and jerky greet me. It's sweet, unlike the bitter smells of the pipes and tobacco Tail Feathers and his people imbibe upon.

I cry into the bounty hunter's clothed chest.

By the time I turn around, my father's body is gone and so is the sheriff. Above us, while the sun rises, my entire world flips.

Someone rubs my back. Those hands massage a trail up and down my spine, causing me to moan and shiver.

The hands stop and rest on my waist. I pull back, swiping at the aftermath of the flood on my face. It's the stormy-eyed cowboy from in front of the sheriff's office.

"I'm sorry about your loss," he says.

"Where did they go?" My voice rasps from sobbing.

"They took him to the undertaker down the street. The sheriff said not to leave town. He'll need to question you."

How had he said all those things and I hadn't heard him?

"My father's d-dead?" It isn't so much a question for him as a reality check for me.

"Man was shot."

With that bit of information, I press my hands to my heart. "Someone killed him."

"Any idea who?"

I shake my head.

"No one threatened him recently?" Those hands trail down my arms and send zings beneath my skin.

"Besides me?" *Did I just confess?* My hand flies up and covers my mouth.

His brows furrow.

Slowly, I uncover my mouth. "I was mad at him, but I didn't mean it. I didn't do this." I try to think who would have done this. Oh, yes! "The gambler! He cheated. My father said so. He was going to go after him. It had to be him."

"What gambler?"

"What time is it?" Oh, this shouldn't be happening.

"The sun's up. Maybe eight or so." He slips his arm around me. "Come on, I'll walk with you to see the sheriff and you can tell me about this gambler."

I don't know why I spill everything to this man even though his name is unknown to me. I feel like I've known him forever, and he's not even the least bit scary to me although a lot of other people might find the gunslinging cowboy intimidating.

When I finish telling him about the poker game, I say, "Maybe you can help me."

"Help you?"

"You can say you're my husband and he'll leave me alone."

The cowboy stops short of the sheriff's office. "I'm only here for my bounty," he says.

Inside the sheriff's office, Sheriff Bently waves another man out. I know the man. He's been in the church on the

Sundays I've been in town. Perhaps Ella Mae will know his name. Not that it's important right at this moment.

Sheriff Bentely offers me a seat. "I'm sorry for your loss, miss. If you sit here a moment, I'll take care of getting Chord his reward and he'll be on his way so we can talk."

"Take your time, Sheriff. The young lady and I have already spoken about what might have happened."

"Using your charm with the ladies again, Chord?" Sheriff Bentely chuckles. He goes over to his desk, signs a wanted poster, and hands it to Chord. "They'll take care of you over at the bank. I don't keep that kind of cash here around criminals."

The bounty hunter takes the wanted poster and rolls it up. He tips his hat my way and heads out of the office. I almost want to call him back. *What for? This man and I hardly know each other.*

"Who was that man?"

"Chord?" Sheriff Bentely takes a seat by the window and looks out on the street. "I'd stay away from the likes of him. You seem like a nice girl. Probably been living out on one of those claims in the mountain panning for gold, am I right?"

"Silver mostly, but yeah. I think it was the gambler who did it." I waste no time letting the sheriff know what I told the bounty hunter and my theory. "My father wasn't in his right mind."

"Most men who drink aren't." He frowns and scratches his chin. "I thought I recognized him. We get a lot of folks passing through Deadwood, but I've locked him up before, I believe. Public drunkenness?"

I don't have it in me to deny it, and lying won't help figure out who did this, although I've already tried and convicted the gambler, Pierce Weston, in my heart.

"My father had a weakness for firewater."

"Those are your ponies hitched to the wagon by the mercantile?"

"Yes." My shoulders slump forward. I got no more tears to shed at this point. My body feels heavy and worn as I sit there.

"I recognize the breed. I take it your father likes to trade with the natives."

I wonder if he's baiting me. There's no law against trading or conversing with the local natives in the mountains. The government created specific places for them to live — a prison with invisible walls.

"We've come across them a few times over the years." Not a lie.

The sheriff nods. "Most people wouldn't care about a drunken prospector getting killed, but since it involves a claim, I'm going to have to insist you don't leave town until we settle this."

"Not leave town?" What would happen if Tail Feathers didn't get his tobacco? Who would make sure no one stole their land? It wasn't wise for one to leave their stake for too long, or another prospector could jump claim on them.

"Would you rather I put you behind bars? Because as of right now, you and this Pierce Weston fellow are the only suspects I have, and it's your word against his."

I sink deeper into my seat. *Can this day get any worse?*

"Sheriff! Sheriff!" Ella Mae, my best friend, rushes into the sheriff's office, her cheeks rosy from racing across town. Her gingham dress twists around her legs as she flings herself toward me. "Oh, Jo. Say it isn't so!" She wraps me up in a bear hug so tight I might not breathe again. Finally, she releases me.

My lungs refill and I can use them again. "It's true. Earl's dead."

"Earl?" This news comes to her as a shock. "Your father is dead?"

"Yeah. Whatever else do you think has happened?"

Ella Mae holds on to me. "My father sent me to fetch you. I thought something happened when I couldn't find you at the boarding house. There is a man waiting for you at the church. He came yesterday, and he's back again today. He says you're going to marry him."

"Over my dead body," I growl.

The sheriff stands and I realize those words came out the wrong way.

"Isn't there some kind of law that a murder suspect can't get married?"

Ella Mae's eyebrows raise clear to her hairline.

Sheriff Bentely scratches his chin and I run for the cell with the biggest lock, begging him to throw away the key.

3

I sit in the cell, arms crossed, leg swinging, and refuse to leave. Ella Mae wrings her hands, torn between staying with me and having to race back to the church to report I am not coming. How many men must a cowgirl leave standing at the altar before she finds the right one?

The year I turned sixteen, I splashed and swam in the creek with Stands With Two Deer and his cousins. That wasn't his name back then. He was Chitto, a word meaning brave in his peoples' tongue. He'd been the boy to kiss me and go exploring with me, and exploring we did. If only Earl knew what went on behind those mountain bushes.

And when Chitto proved himself a man, he brought me those two ponies. I took them, fed them, and the next morning he tried to take me to his lodging and make me his wife.

I wasn't about to let any man think they could buy me. I offered to give the horses back, but Earl took them, stiffing Chitto a bride.

Besides, Earl needed me. Who would wash his socks and brew the coffee? It didn't matter I could swing a pickaxe and help sift for precious metals like silver and gold. Momma left him, and he wasn't about to let me leave, too.

Except now Earl is gone.

And Chitto isn't the boy pulling me behind bushes to steal kisses anymore. He is Stands With Two Deer, a name given to him at manhood, a name meaning a man with two wives. It didn't take him long to catch another pony and lure in another bride. While I didn't believe in divorce, I didn't believe in polygamy either.

I'm a one man kind of woman.

With the coast clear and the gambler gone, I let Ella Mae yank me from the cell. Sheriff Bentely wouldn't leave me locked inside. He's got a murderer to hunt down and a gambler to investigate.

If not for the way we met, I might find the gambler hard to resist. If I'm a betting gal, which I'm not, I'd put all my stakes in the gambler's guilt. It's not right of me to judge him before he has a chance to prove himself innocent. Where I really need to go is to take care of my dear departed father.

It puts a weight on my shoulders, and I can't help feeling dragged down the closer we approach the church.

Outside on the stairs waiting for me is Pierce Weston, the gambler.

"And here I thought you were getting all prettied up for our wedding, darling. No difference, the preacher is waiting inside." He's dressed in a different suit, navy and pinstripes with the same silver vest. His boots shine like his eyes with the excitement of a small child given a cookie right before supper.

Ella Mae leans in close. "He's handsome."

"Then *you* marry him," I whisper back.

Ella Mae breaks out in a fit of giggles. She's more dressed to become a bride today than me. She always looks so womanly in her cheery yellow gingham and dark honey hair.

Spots of pink dot her cheeks. I know for certain she's considering it, although she's got a beau.

She isn't wrong. The gambler has this twinkle in his eye, and my belly flops in the best of ways. I shake my head, remembering what got us here. Earl threw my marital status in the pot. The gambler doesn't seem the type who would tie himself down with a wife. He probably heard gold mine and saw dollar signs. Thanks to Earl, he might get his hands on it—the land, not the gold.

I have to figure out a way to stop him.

"There isn't going to be a wedding today." I keep my tone sharp so he knows I mean business.

The gambler sets those calculating emerald eyes on me. A man who dresses to the nines and plays cards in the afternoons must do this for a living. What would he want with a mine claim, anyway? I try to imagine him hunched down, sifting through the dirt for precious metals, and all I see are those gorgeous green eyes of his.

"Jo's father passed," Ella Mae explains.

The gambler steps down from the church stairs and reaches for me. His eyes widen and his voice fills with concern. "That's why you didn't make it to the dress shop and why you're late? Oh, darlin', you should have said so. We can go get that dress now and have you looking prettier than a meadow by noon. We'll have a celebratory lunch, and I've reserved a room for us at the hotel."

Is he for real? "My father is dead."

I'm still numb with the news. My head pounds with one of those headaches you get after crying. Can't the man see I've probably got tears staining down my cheeks? Maybe not since I wiped them all on the bounty hunter's shirt. The thought of Chord with his arms around me makes my blood warm. I shouldn't even be thinking of him on a first name basis.

"I know, darling. There's nothing we can do now about

that, can we? He'd want you to move on. We'll talk to the good reverend and arrange for him to say a few words at the burial. Don't you worry about anything. As your husband I'll take care of everything."

"That's awful nice, isn't it, Jo?" Ella Mae sways and smiles. She's fallen under a trance for those emerald eyes. Part of me wants to remind her about the guy who stole her heart, but I've got bigger concerns at the moment.

"It should be, seeing as he's the one who done it."

The gambler steps back, looking offended. "You don't think I had anything to do with your father's death, do you?"

I cross my arms and level my meanest glare at him. "I don't think. I know."

The gambler's shoulders roll back, and his eyes harden. "You have proof?"

"I don't need proof. I know you did it." Just like that, a few more tears slip free, and I reach up to swipe them away.

"You ought to be careful accusing people of doing things without proof. Isn't that right, sheriff?" The gambler looks past me.

Sheriff Bentely must have followed me when Ella Mae and I left his office.

"You must be the gambler." Sheriff Bentely straightens his gold star on his shirt pocket.

"Gambler, huh?" He glances my way and winks. The man is totally incorrigible. Ella Mae giggles again. I cross my arms and roll my eyes.

"Pierce Weston," the gambler introduces himself.

"I'm sorry to interrupt your wedding plans. I promise I won't keep you long, but I'm going to need to ask you a few questions."

"Shoot," he says, then realizes his blunder. "Sorry, Sheriff. Ask me whatever you wish. I have nothing to hide." He holds up his hands to show he's not armed. I have a feeling this gambler likes to keep a few cards hidden. No tricks are going to get him out of this one.

"Anything?" Ella Mae dives right in, acting so coy. It makes me smile. Next, she'll be batting her lashes at him and forgetting about the ranch hand on the Triple D.

I give her a pinch to bring her out of it.

"Ow." She rubs her elbow and glowers at me. "Jolene Willow Dean, that's just mean."

"Tell it to your cowboy when he comes calling on Sunday," I hiss at her.

She turns, a little peaked, points that nose of hers up in the air, and marches off into the church. "I'm going to go tell Father what's going on."

I hurt her feelings. As I think to go after her, I can feel the gambler's gaze on me. I meet his stare. Slowly, a smile spreads across his face, with dimples to boot. A girl could get lost between those dimples, which is why I snap myself out of it.

I bet this man knows how to manipulate women. I sure am not falling for it, or him! He killed my father, and that one thought alone is enough to strike the flame of justice burning deep in my gut.

"What?" I snap as he hasn't stopped staring and the sheriff, too. An eyebrow raises as he says my name, "Jolene."

There ought to be a law against a man saying a woman's name like that. Too bad my belly is already full of heat, and it's not the kind to go away soon.

"Everyone calls me Jo. I prefer it that way." There is something too intimate in the way it sounds when he says it.

"Ah, but it's a pretty name for the woman who's going to become my wife."

"It will be hard to get married if you're in jail," it comes out as a low growl. "Arrest him, Sheriff. Take him down and put him in that cell and lock him away. Throw away the key."

"Come now, Jo," the sheriff says. "What happened to your

father was a terrible thing." He addresses the gambler, "Why don't you give the young lady a few days to bury her father and then see to the wedding? It's not like she's going anywhere soon."

The gambler's lips flatline but he agrees. He steps close to me, tweaks my chin, and says, "The sheriff's right. We'll take care of seeing to your father first, then make no mistake, my darling Jolene, we will be wed." He pats his suit jacket. Some might have thought he touched his heart, but the crinkle of the paper under the fabric tells me he's up to no good.

He's no different from Stands With Two Deer or any other man I've met, sans one. I haven't made my mind up about the bounty hunter Chord. Who knows if our paths will ever cross again? A bigger part than I wish to admit saddens at the thought.

I watch the gambler walk off with the sheriff. Ella Mae returns from inside the church and hooks her hand through my arm. "It's just as well. Father says it was a bad day for a wedding anyway. He's going to head out to the Larson farm and check on their family. They caught some sickness and haven't been into town for weeks to attend church."

Most folks hadn't been into church for weeks after that last spring blizzard we got. I say nothing as she goes on about needing a dress and borrowing a blue ribbon. I can hear in her voice the romanticism of it all as she envisions me marrying the gambler.

Perhaps if circumstances were different. One man has already betrayed me, two if you count my father. I'm not about to let another man decide for me or treat me like second best. My heart feels heavier than ever. I can't imagine having any more room in it for disappointment or loss.

I head to the mercantile with Ella Mae. While Mr. Jensen is sympathetic to my recent loss, he says I can pick up my supplies when I'm ready to leave town. Thanks to my father, and now Jensen, I haven't got a cent left to my name.

Hank lets me stable the ponies and park my wagon out back. "It's in decent shape. You could sell it," he says.

I politely refuse. I need that wagon to get those supplies back to the claim. Another thing I have to take care of seeing that Earl put me in this position. I should feel relieved he's gone. Instead, I'm overwhelmed with the prospect of getting out of the mess he's put me in.

By lunch, Ella Mae needs to race back to her house to help her mother. She offers for me to come, and I think about the gambler's offer. No doubt about it, I'd rather spend time with Ella Mae.

Pearl Carter makes a mean stew, and she's the one who taught me to make biscuits. We sit at the table waiting for her to finish her meal prayer. She's a short woman with golden hair which she always keeps twisted in the back. She's got on the same color gingham dress as Ella Mae, and I know the rest of the Carter sisters have them on, too. Ella Mae is one of five girls blessed in the Carter family. Poor Reverend Carter is going to have his hands full trying to keep them all pure before marriage. The eldest, Mary Sue, ran off last spring with a young buck passing through. The news floated clear up into the mountain, seeing it was the good reverend's daughter who disappeared into the night. She left a note, and occasionally a letter comes in the mail.

"I'm sorry about your father," Pearl says, sipping her soup.

"It will take the undertaker a day or so to get the coffin ready. We can bury him as soon as it's ready." Reverend Carter joins us before his journey.

In the next room, Ella Mae's three younger sisters work on their embroidery and sketches by the big picture window.

"What will you do?" Pearl asks.

I shrug.

"Jo can't leave town. Sheriff told her to stick around a few days while he tries to find out who killed her father and settle their claim." Ella Mae says it loud enough for her sisters to hear.

"That's good. I feared you'd try to go back up to that claim of your father's and be all alone. It's not good to be up there alone."

What Pearl means to say is it's not good for a woman to be alone without protection of a man. I can see it plain in her face and the way her eyes avert to her husband.

"Oh, Jo, I just had a thought. You can stay here with us," Ella Mae says.

She shares a room with two of her sisters.

"Thank you, but I have a room at the boarding house."

Ella Mae taps her spoon on her bowl. "You paid in advance? Because didn't Mr. Jensen keep your money for supplies and Earl lost it all in the card game yesterday?"

Leave it to Ella Mae to pay attention and spill it all out in front of the reverend.

He reaches across and pats Ella's hand. "I believe Jolene has a beau who will see that she's taken care of."

Pearl perks up and her eyes land on me. "A man? Is he calling on you?"

Ella Mae's sisters come pouring into the kitchen. It's small and tidy, but they must eat their meals in shifts, as there isn't enough seating at the table for all of them.

"He won her in a card game. Seems Earl ensured she would be taken care of after all." Reverend Carter got up from the table. "We should move up that wedding before the funeral because of circumstances."

Circumstances? The gambler said he'd gotten us a hotel room. Oh my. *Oh no!*

"A card game? You can't marry off this girl because of a

bet in a card game! Why that's... That's..." Pearl sputters to complete her thoughts aloud

I shake my head. "Oh, I'm not marrying him. He killed my father, and I'm going to prove it."

"It's not right for a woman your age to be alone." Reverend Carter frowns. Sometimes I wonder if the man is getting hard of hearing. Pearl said the same thing before him.

While they might both agree it isn't right for a woman to be forced into marriage over a card game, I can tell from the look on Pearl's face and Reverend Carter's frown I would be preaching to the choir.

In the meantime, I have a father to bury, a claim to secure, and a killer to put behind bars.

4

Proving Pierce Weston, a.k.a. the gambler, killed my father is turning out to be harder than I thought. There are no witnesses to my father's shooting, and as loud as it got in the saloon on a Friday night, no one heard a thing. Cowboys come in shooting it up at night with excitement and too much firewater in their veins.

My only hope is Amaryllis. This time of day, I know I'll find the woman sitting in her room above the saloon, putting on her paint and a different colored gown to prepare for the Saturday night crowd. I can't imagine them coming back and celebrating again for a second night after all the whooping it up the night before, but they will.

I check with the bartender, a stout fellow named Glen, who watches me with beady little eyes like a rat while he cleans glasses to stick under the bar.

A few afternoon geezers sit at the end of the bar and another handful at a table. I know for a fact these cowboys are up to no good. Everyone knows the ranch bosses go to the hotel dining room to discuss business. I don't care about their shady shenanigans and rap my knuckles on the door again after a few minutes.

Robbie lets me in, and Amaryllis shoos him off for us to speak. I notice a cot at the end of the bed where Robbie sleeps when his ma isn't entertaining guests.

When she motions for me to sit on the edge of the bed, I prefer to stand. I meant no disrespect, but I have a good idea of what has gone on atop that mattress and can't in right conscience sit on it.

Amaryllis paints her eyelids and watches me from the mirror. "What can I do for you, Toots?"

"My father's dead." Those words sound so hollow coming out of me. An entire day has almost gone by, and I feel as if I have been going through the motions waiting to wake up from a dream since the scary part passed. Or has it?

The gambler comes to mind, and those emerald eyes of his flash in my memory sending a trickle down my spine. One shouldn't like the way a man looks when he's a murderer.

"I thought it might be him this morning behind the saloon. Robbie found the body." She pushes out her lips and smears a streak of red across them. "Poor kid. Good thing he's getting older and will be off on his own soon."

I clasp my hands together. Sometimes I wish I'd been born a boy. Then Earl couldn't have got me in this predicament. No matter, there are advantages to having a woman's perspective on things. I feel bad for Robbie, but his mother is right. In a few years he can apprentice with Jensen, or I know he spies on Hank like the rest of us. Only Robbie has different reasons. He actually *wants to learn* the blacksmith trade. As for the rest of us, we just want to watch the blacksmith at work.

"Now, I know you don't have a momma anymore. Heard she ran off with some cowboy headed to Tucson a while ago. I'm guessing you came because old Ruby is a prude, and you want to know what to expect when that handsome gambling man takes you back to his hotel room and really makes you his wife." Amaryllis winks.

It sends a flare of heat up my neck, hits my cheeks, and burns clear to the tips of my ears. It hadn't crossed my mind. Not one bit. Okay, maybe once, but I'd quickly shove any thoughts of what happened behind closed doors with married people aside. I can't even consider the gambler for a moment in that way.

On second thought, it made me wonder if he would kiss me gentle-like, or rough as I imagine the bounty hunter would. Not that I hadn't been kissed by Stands With Two Deer. Oh Lord, did that make me a tainted woman?

I slap my hand to my cheek, hoping to get my face to cool back down.

Amaryllis chuckles and touches up the kohl around her eyes. She is beautiful, with a heart-shaped face and long, sweeping lashes.

Looking at myself in her mirror makes me feel plain. Why would the gambler insist on hitching himself to the likes of me?

Amaryllis stands. "Well, I suppose we should get started."

"Get started?" An instant alarm tells me to run. I plant my boot heels on the floor as Amaryllis giggles again.

"I'll keep it simple. Did you get a dress? You have a dress, don't you?"

What was it with everyone wanting me to have a dress? I shake my head.

Amaryllis taps her cheek and tilts her head. "I could put you in one of mine. Would you like me to look?"

"No, I'm good. Ella Mae offered me a dress for church tomorrow, but I won't be needing one."

"Oh, I see. You don't think you're that kind of girl, uh?" She pushes a lock of hair from her face. "Consider yourself lucky, Toots. Your father may have lost in the gamble, but at least he was looking out for you." She tucks another lock of hair into place.

"Hardly," I mutter.

Amaryllis gives me a long, hard stare and presses her thin lips together. Reaching for a brush to dust her cheeks, she shrugs. "Well, if it doesn't work out with the gambler, you've got the looks. You could make a buck or two here with me, or the dancing hall over in Silver Valley."

"Thanks, but no."

"Got your sights set on the gambler? I wouldn't go getting hitched in those pants! Not to a man like Pierce Weston." Her eyelashes flutter. I could practically hear her heart thumping for the gambler. Or maybe it was mine?

But she knows his name. As good a sign as any. I push forward, feeling awkward where this impromptu visit on my part has gone. "I'm not planning on getting married."

She waves off my words. "A handsome devil as that? You are a lucky girl, Jo. You don't want to end up dancing in Silver Valley, then take my advice and marry Mr. Weston." She reaches around me to the bed and tugs a black lace shawl off the end.

"I need to find who killed my father."

She wraps the shawl around herself and shivers. Not that it is cold inside the saloon. I could imagine all kinds of sinful things going on here to heat the place up.

Amaryllis turns away. I watch for her reaction. "My father said the gambler cheated. You saw his cards, didn't you?"

"I saw him pull the ace, Toots."

"You were watching the game. Surely you saw more than that?"

Amaryllis adjusts her bodice and heads for the door. She holds it open and motions for me to go out ahead of her. "I might have, but it wasn't his cards I was most interested in last night. You know what I'm talking about?"

What little heat cools from my face flares again. Amaryllis smiles, tucking her shawl back against her arms. Her assets are the first one notices when they look at her.

My eyes drift down to the sisters, and I stop myself there. No comparison. I step out past the saloon matron.

"You think he could have cheated?"

"I think we are all capable of cheating. Did you look at the man? He's from out east, or maybe it was Mississippi. I think I heard him say something about a riverboat."

"You saw him leave. Did he come back? Did my father come back?"

Her eyes fill with loss, her grief most likely coming from the loss of the gambler and his deep pockets than my father's exit from this earth. "Not that I saw, but I was pretty busy. Pierce said he was heading to get the preacher. I figured you were all off getting that settled. Wasn't Reverend Carter around? Well, don't you worry, he'll be there tomorrow. It's Sunday."

The fact Amaryllis knows the gambler on a first name basis cools my flesh and sinks a brick in my stomach.

Of course a woman in Amaryllis's profession would have gotten to know quite a few men. I should have figured a man like the gambler would be no stranger to the ladies.

Another reason I would be wise to avoid him.

"If you get cold feet, send him my way, will you?"

"Sure thing." I follow her down the hall.

"You shouldn't let that one escape," she says as she departs down the stairs and into the saloon. Outside, the late afternoon sun warms the windows.

I have no intentions of letting my gambling man get away. I shouldn't think of him as mine. The man is dangerous in more ways than one, and I plan on making sure he gets what he deserves. The only commitments he's making in the future are twenty to life at the gray bar hotel. I snicker, thinking of the fancy pants gambler getting his hands dirty.

Since Hank has my wagon as collateral, Jensen has the money on account for my supplies, and Earl lost our hard-earned cash in a hand of cards, I have one more place to visit. Ruby agreed I could stay at the boarding house, but I have to work for the nights extra I stay. All I have left is the old spitfire rifle of my father's.

Normally, my father carried it or kept it in the wagon for safekeeping. I keep it tucked under my bed at the boarding house. The bullets are in the nightstand by the bed. Ruby moved me to a smaller room no bigger than the water closet. It has a cot and a nightstand with a pitcher on top. I suppose I should be grateful to have any place to sleep at all. Not that I need much room, and the cost is cheaper per night. Since it is located around the corner of the stairs, no one would know I was there.

As much as I want to go to that room, fall onto the bed, and let my mind and my body rest after the day, I have yet to visit the undertaker. A shiver creeps down my spine thinking of seeing Earl's dead body laid out in a pine box.

Frank Harrison wears a patch on one eye, with a clean white scar straight down from it. His weathered face and grim expression sends a person's internal instincts to fight or flight. He isn't tall and lean or even old, as one would expect. The man has three crooked fingers and a curve in his spine. The suspenders from his pants hang down over his hips and keep his arms covered in a sweatstain down his back. He works under the roof extended from his shop. Covering my nose with my hand, I approach him.

"I'm here about my father's body." I force the ball of sorrow down my throat.

"I'll have his coffin ready tomorrow." He spits off into the dirt. Glancing at me, he says, "Took you long enough to get

here. That husband of yours took care of the cost. The boys
are already out digging."

A breeze comes through the openings where there should
have been walls giving a moment of fresh air. A smile flits on
my face, thinking maybe a breath of fresh air is a sign things
will go right from here on out.

Frank grunts, picks up his handsaw, and nods to the shop
behind him. "He's in there. Don't bother going through his
pockets. They're empty."

"You went through my father's pockets?" What kind of
person goes through a dead man's pockets?

Frank wipes his nose, squinting at me from his one eye.
"You'll have to ask the sheriff and that husband of yours."

"Oh." A feeling of depletion releases from me. The tight-
ness in my chest twists as I leave Frank to head inside the shop.

"The bodies are in the back," he calls.

I haven't ever seen a dead body laid out for viewing. Once
in Tail Feather's village, Chitto allowed me to witness one of
their ceremonies for burning the dead. No matter how many
years it's been, he'll always be my Chitto and not Stands With
Two Deer. That day, Chitto squished me between his pals
Falling Rock and Yellow Cat, or at least that was the best
translation I could give. I watched as one of the older
warriors of their tribe was taken to the burial grounds. The
people of their tribe believe a man needs his horse, his
weapons, and a meal to take to the other side. They raised the
body, wrapped in a beautifully woven blanket on stilts. I
remember I cried, for the horse mostly. I didn't know the man
who died, but something inside me didn't feel it was right to
kill an innocent animal. Chitto tried to console me. He told
me the horse would have died without its caretaker. I didn't
believe it.

I'd been a stupid girl then, not knowing the genuine pain of
death. I still didn't. All I know is that someone shot my father,

and while they might have shot him, they left an even bigger hole inside of me.

A hole so large I never would have guessed the man I despised these last few years could cause such grief to me now.

Thankfully, inside, my father isn't hard to find. There are two other bodies inside their respective pine coffins and the lids halfway down. Not bothering to look, I go to Earl and immediately frown.

Where is his left shoe?

If not for the dark stain on his shirt, I would have thought him sleeping. Earl never was a peaceful sleeper.

Glancing around the room, I slip my hand against his arm. "It's not him," I whisper. "He's not here anymore."

I curl my fingers as I reach and uncurl them to slide down over his shirt pocket, which couldn't contain anything because the fabric laid down, torn.

Upon closer inspection, my father's face has a purple and green discoloration around his right eye and his chin. He'd gotten in a scuffle with someone. Had he and the gambler got in a fight? The wheels turn in my head. Of course they fought. Then the gambler pulled out a gun.

A few stray tears trickle down my cheeks, clogging my throat as the ball of sorrow slips up on me.

"You old coot. I warned you not to go drowning in the firewater."

I pat his pocket and go to reach in when I hear boots approaching. Peering over my shoulder, I jerk my hand back. "What are you still doing here?"

The bounty hunter presses his shoulder into the door frame of the back room. "I think the better question, Dimples, is what are you doing?"

The man makes me quiver in ways I didn't know I could. "What am I doing? My father is here. He's dead and I've got to arrange for his burial. And I had to see him. I couldn't let them nail his coffin shut without saying goodbye. What kind of daughter do you think I am?"

Those stone-cold gray eyes met mine. "Calm down. Dead men don't talk."

"What's that supposed to mean?" Is he accusing me of something? Gosh, do I look guilty?

"Exactly what I said." He reaches inside that long jacket and pulls out a slip of paper. "Sheriff asked me to give you this."

"The sheriff asked you?" I'm hesitant to take it.

"He rode out to the Triple D to talk to a cowboy who might know what happened." The bounty hunter nods toward the body behind me. Tempted as I am to ask how many other bodies lying here are put in this state by him, I press my lips tight together. It is an old photo, a torn piece of a family album. I recognize the face of the woman who gave birth to me. My father carried this torn photograph in his boot. He always said he planned to keep my mother close to his boot because if she ever came back, he'd make her kiss his feet before he gave her the left boot on his foot.

The one that is missing.

"Thank you. Still not sure why the sheriff would have you deliver this."

"I told him I would."

"How did you know where to look?"

"It's what I do."

"Oh." I stare down at the photo. "I didn't think you would stick around once you got your reward money."

Not that I am complaining. The bounty hunter isn't hard to look at. Under all that rough exterior, there has to be a sweet, caring part he hid. A part I wonder if I search for long enough, I will find.

Realizing where my thoughts have gone, I whirl around. Between him and the gambler, I have blushed and cried more than I have in a decade. I'd have a lot to atone for the next day. I promised Ella Mae I'd sit with her at church.

"Some rewards are worth waiting for." He pushes away from the door frame. "You shouldn't linger here. It's not good to dwell with the dead." His words come out soft.

I spread my hands on my father's stiff leg and stare at that one boot on his foot. The one with the hole nearly worn through. "He's missing a shoe," I say. "Don't you think that's odd?"

The bounty hunter steps close beside me, his sweet tobacco smell tickling at my nose. My heart races a little.

"Maybe."

I pull off the sock without thinking, nothing there. Either my father has swapped feet or… I didn't hesitate. I grab the boot and start unlacing.

"What are you doing?"

"My father had a habit of keeping things in his boots."

"Like his feet?"

"Like this…" I tug off the boot with the bounty hunter's help, almost gag at the smell of rotted toe fungus, and peel down the sock.

"You were saying?"

I pick up the boot, shake it.

Nothing.

"It was in the other boot," I say.

"What?" Poor man doesn't have a clue.

"Whatever the killer wanted."

5

I skip supper and spend the night in my room. There's a pink dress on the bed and a note from Ella Mae. *Mary left this when she ran off. Momma thought it might fit you for church tomorrow.* I hold up the short-sleeved dress as if it were a dish rag. It's pink with a lace ruffle around the neckline. Several pleats are in the waist, but it takes a lot of squishing and tucking to get the sisters to keep from popping out. For a tall girl like me, the dress is too short. I'm a head taller than most of the Carter sisters. At least my boots come up to my calves and cover what the dress doesn't. If I were still a girl in the schoolyard, no one would say a thing, but I am not. I am a full-grown woman.

When it's time for church, I pull back my shoulders and wretch open the door. I come face to face with a wide chest blocking my way and stone-cold eyes breaking up a little in surprise. A man's eyes are said to be the window to his soul. The ones looking into mine blink and close the gate on what might have been a second of compassion. They're disturbing just the same. Not like those glinting emeralds of the gambler man, but penetrating as if it's my soul, my heart getting probed.

"Let me guess, you came to track me down again?" I pull my door shut. It isn't his business to see my tiny room or my pants laying on the bed.

"Don't flatter yourself, Dimples. I'm headed to breakfast. I hear the lady of the house makes a mean pot of porridge and if you're early, you might grab a slice of bacon."

"My name isn't Dimples, it's Jo. '

"Jo." He steps back, taking in my pink dress, and my face heats to match. I cross my arms, self-conscious about the sisters getting loose. Maybe I can find Ella Mae and borrow a shawl. I'm half tempted to put my shirt back on over top. On second thought, that is what I plan to do.

"Doesn't suit. Dimples is better."

"Dimples?" No one has ever called me by a nickname before. Once Chitto said I should have a tribal name, as his so-called wife, he used my middle name, Willow. Having a nickname from a man seems inappropriate, especially given the circumstances. I have known him for a day.

"Look in the mirror. You'll see what I mean."

I take him up on the offer, only because I want to grab my shirt and pull it on. I don't have a mirror, but the window reflects this time of morning and I stare for a long moment. Dimples. Yep, I have them. When I smile, they make me look so much younger than I am. The last thing I want is this man thinking I'm a girl.

Why should I care?

I do. I want him to see me as a woman. A strong woman.

I tug my shirt over the sisters, leaving it open a bit, and sigh. There is a chill in the air coming down from the mountains. I see it through the window in my room. It's unlikely the day is going to get any warmer. Foolishly, I left my jacket up on our claim. My shirt will do. I take one last look in the mirror.

I'm not here to impress anyone.

Well, maybe it wouldn't hurt to undo these braids. I look like an oversized schoolgirl, so I do.

Back out in the hall, he's gone.

"Well, don't you look pretty for church this morning." Ruby stands with her hand on her hip and a pot of coffee in the other. She raises the coffee and I take her up on the offer. Thanks to the bounty hunter, I've got bacon on the brain.

From the first moment I ever stepped into her house as a young girl with double braids, Ruby has always had a way of knowing what I needed.

"I saved one for you," she says, taking me in. Without another word, she shakes her head, and heads off into the dining room to feed the other boarders.

Outside, the streets are quiet. People walk to church and a few horses trot on by. Deadwood isn't usually such a quiet little town. I imagine the cowboys have all ridden back to their ranch or gone home to their claims if they're not sleeping off the weekend activities here in town. Ruby has no tolerance for the rowdy bunch. Most of them find a place at Warner's Hotel, the Swanson sisters, or stay passed out at the saloon.

There isn't an establishment in town open on the Sabbath until the lunch crowd.

I find Ella Mae in church sitting front and center with her beau Lincoln. He must have shaved off the beard after the long winter. Throughout service, he runs his hand on the smoothness of his chin. Ella Mae watches that hand, and I figure she's counting down the minutes for her father's sermon to end so she can pull him away somewhere private to test out the smoothness around those lips. There isn't a part of me that doesn't envy her. By the end of summer I'll probably come back into town and find them married.

Lincoln holds his cowboy hat on his lap and keeps his eyes on Reverend Carter. I have a feeling he knows the reverend keeps an eye on him. Or maybe it's the sermon. According to the good reverend, we're all going to experience a heat wave if we don't change our ways, and it won't be from the weather.

Ella Mae leans into me and whispers, "Are you trying to stir up gossip?"

"No."

"Well, you've done it." She wiggles back on the hard wooden seat of the pew.

"Done what?" I hiss, and suddenly Pearl leans forward from the other side of Lincoln. Her scolding look makes me clamp my lips together.

Ella Mae waits a moment, until Reverend Carter's voice rises higher in his conviction, and whispers in my ear, "Killed your father."

"You know I didn't."

Lincoln leans in, pressing his finger to his lips. He bows his head and I realize we're supposed to be praying. I huff, squeezing my eyes shut tight, and Reverend Carter's words become a blockade behind the storm of my own thoughts. *Lord, please don't let the gambler get away with murder. He can't take our hard-earned claim. Please protect Tail Feather's tribe. They don't deserve to have to stay cooped up on that reservation all day.* I squint and look over at Lincoln, sliding his hand toward Ella Mae. *Don't make me get married either, at least unless I choose.* I sigh with an amen.

Somehow, I can't picture myself married to the gambling man, nor can I picture him with dirt on his hands working our mine. What's a man like him want with my father's claim, anyway?

Probably thinks he can sell it. Guys like him are always after cash, cold hard cash, or at least I think they are.

Soon, the congregation is filing out of the church. As I'm in line to make my way out, I see Grace, who owns the dress shop, is looking at me. She's got her golden tresses pulled back and coiled in a bun. The way her eyes are fluttering up and down has me closing my shirt more. No sooner do I take a step forward than I catch the scent of yeast. When I glance back, Pearl, Ella Mae's mother, is behind me.

She rests her hand on my arm and leans in. "Don't you worry none. I'll speak to Grace, and we'll get that gown altered to fit."

As squished as the sisters are, I doubt any amount of altering is going to fix this dress.

Outside, I catch up with Ella Mae, who is speaking with Hannah Baker and Lottie Larson. Beside Lincoln is a familiar bounty hunter. My insides twist and, before I can reach them, another familiar figure blocks my path.

"Don't tell me this is the dress my money bought." Pierce Weston holds out his arms widely. There is no side-stepping the gambler.

"You don't like it?"

He gets this sideways grin as his arms lower. His hands take me by the arms, and I know that look. It must be universal. Those lids hang low, and he leans in. Leaning back, I glance around, hoping for some help.

Hannah and Lottie gaze my way, and soon they have the attention of Ella Mae, and even Grace is watching.

"Pink isn't your color, darlin', but don't you worry. It's what's underneath that counts. Come on, the preacher is here and so are we. We've got plenty of witnesses, and when it's all done, we'll go see the dressmaker together. The wife of Pierce Weston should have the latest fashion befitting a woman of her status."

What's underneath? Status? My brows furrow together. Suddenly, things are feeling a little drafty. "I've got to go."

As I head in her direction, Ella Mae waves and tries to go around the gambler. She has her arm around Lincoln. But the gambler is not letting go. Oh no, he's pinning those sparkling emerald eyes on me like a prize turkey in fall. Under any other circumstances, I might feel flattered. However, there is the little matter of my father's death and the fact I very much believe he's the killer.

"Now, wait one minute, darlin'." He says, "darlin' with a roll of the 'r'. The man is a player, and it makes my knees a little weak. Of course, if my dress got any shorter above the boots, folks might think I took a job at the saloon.

"I told you, I'm not marrying you!"

Ella Mae, along with the posse of Hannah, Lottie, Lincoln, and the bounty hunter, head our way.

"I missed you last night." Pierce's expression changes. "I left an invitation for dinner with the woman who runs the boarding house."

Lottie and Hannah have stars in their eyes, and I can't help noticing how Lottie has snuggled up close to the bounty hunter. She's got no right getting close to the man.

"I didn't get it." I don't owe him an explanation, nor is it Ruby's job to deliver messages.

"Then you won't mind having lunch with me over at the hotel. Of course, we could go talk to the preacher and make it a wedding lunch. I still have a room reserved for us at the hotel."

"The woman's father isn't even in the ground yet." The bounty hunter stands beside me. Lottie puts a fist on her hip. Hannah whispers something about my dress. All I catch is "pink" and "look at her boots."

"And who are you?" Pierce puffs up his chest. He yanks on my arm and keeps me close.

"Chord Townes." The bounty hunter tips his hat up. His voice doesn't cease to make my heart thump a little harder.

"He's a lawman," Lottie says. She's dressed in green, and her dark hair is twisted up in the back beneath her floral bonnet. She's slim and the shortest of us three women.

"He's a bounty hunter," I correct and smugly add, "Go

ahead. Leave town. He'll hunt you down and drag you back here for killing my father."

Pierce barks a laugh. "The only one doing any killing around here, darlin', is you."

Everyone around us gasps.

"Me?" I point to myself.

"You are making me wait to marry you. You're killin' me, darlin'." He presses his hand to his chest and winces. Now all three ladies look as if they'll swoon at his declaration.

It's by the scent of sweet tobacco that I keep from rolling my eyes.

"You wound me," he says. "I won you fair and square in that card game. I had no reason to wish your father ill."

And just like that, Pierce has everyone's vote of innocence. He invites folks to join us at the hotel for lunch. Surprisingly, the bounty hunter comes along.

As we pass Grace's shop, I pause a moment to check out the dress she's got in the window. It's dark blue with a waistcoat. Far too fancy for anything I'd ever wear.

Lincoln sits by the bounty hunter, and I hear him talking about his latest bounty. I try to remain ladylike when the server comes to take our orders. I've got my mind made up on the fried chicken with mashed potatoes and gravy, except Pierce doesn't give me a chance. He orders for both of us: fresh trout caught from a nearby stream this morning. The nearest stream is twenty miles away. I wrinkle my nose and exchange looks with Ella. Lottie and Hannah sit between the bounty hunter and the gambler on the other side of the table. They're so enamored by the bounty hunter they don't even notice they've got their elbows on the tabletop.

Throughout lunch, I pick at the trout. The limp greens beside it aren't any more appealing. Ella Mae and Lincoln are the first to go, and when it comes time to pay the bill, the bounty hunter is the one to pay.

Pierce stands when I do. He places his arm out for me to take. "What's the matter? I don't bite."

"Maybe she's a little wary of taking the arm of a man who might have killed her father," Chord, the bounty hunter, says, Lottie and Hannah on either side of him.

Hannah grins at him, laying her hand on his arm, and teeters out a fan of giggles. "Oh, please. Everyone knows Jo isn't afraid of anything. Living out there on that claim alone with her father. Surely a man like Mr. Weston doesn't scare you?"

I guffaw at the thought while a quiver starts down in my belly. More than a quiver, it's like that time I got trapped down in the mine and Earl took way too long to get me out.

"Is it hot in here?" I wave my hand to fan myself and take a deep breath, hoping they get the hint we should leave.

"How about we take a ride out and you can show me that claim I now own?"

"It's a day's ride," I say.

The bounty hunter pulls back his duster, and I wonder if he ever sheds it. "You're not to leave town."

"You the sheriff?" Pierce challenges.

"Don't make me track you." And with those words, the bounty hunter turns and takes Lottie and Hannah with him. What I wouldn't do to have positions reversed.

"Well, then…" Pierce clears his throat. "A walk then around town?"

The last thing I need is to strut around town anymore in this getup. The sisters have been begging to breathe for at least an hour. I shake my head. "I need to return to the boarding house. You can walk me there."

And he does.

At the door, he takes my hand and looks deep into my eyes. "I know you don't trust me. I wouldn't trust me either, but if it makes you feel better about me and about our upcoming nuptials, then I'll prove to you I had nothing to do with your father's murder."

"How do you plan to do that?"

He squeezes my hands, leans in, and my breath catches in my throat. "I'm going to talk to the sheriff. I'll offer a reward in order to find out information that can help find the killer. I hope that will ease your mind."

Isn't that what a guilty person does? I'm convinced even more that the gambler has an ulterior motive. I'll have to spend more time with him if I'm going to discover what card he plans to pull next.

6

My father's burial is a silent affair. Reverend Carter reads from the Bible. Above us, the sky is a dark gray and, judging by the view toward the mountains, it's even darker in that direction.

I swapped my pink dress for my pants. Ella Mae has my arm as we stand in front of my father's grave. I've got no more tears to shed. I'm numb, standing there, holding a handful of dirt in my hands.

Ella Mae rests her head against me. "I'm sorry, Jolene. But you got to know you're not alone. You don't have to go back up that mountain. You can stay here. So what if the killer is found or not? It won't bring your father back."

No. It won't bring my father back. And as ornery as Earl was, he still deserves justice. Plus, once I prove the gambler is guilty of murder, then I won't have to worry about losing our claim. Stands With Two Deer will be safe and so will Tail Feathers and the rest of his people. They're counting on me to return. It's about time I focus on the task at hand. I don't want to be stuck in this dead-end town any more than I want to marry a man with ulterior motives. A man I hardly know. It breaks my heart. My father would throw me away in a card game as easily as he threw away our claim. There has to be another reason.

Firewater makes people do stupid things.

"There is more to this." I turn and look at Ella Mae. "I have to know."

"Welcome to Deadwood. Saturday night shoot outs are a thing."

"They took his boot." And I tell Ella Mae everything I know, leaving out about Stands With Two Deer and the agreement my father made with Tail Feathers. How long are they going to wait for their promised supplies?

"You don't know what happened, Jo. You need to leave this to the sheriff. Lincoln says that bounty hunter guy, Townes, he's brought in the worst of the criminals. He always gets his guy. You should hire him to find your father's killer. That way you're not putting yourself in danger."

"That's just it," I tell her, slightly embarrassed. "I don't got nothing to offer. Thanks to Earl, I'm broke."

"You can't be that broke. You're staying at Ruby's, and you paid for those supplies."

"Yeah, with the money I got from the gambler. He told me to buy a dress."

Slowly, I see Ella Mae put it all together. She gives me a hug. "It's all going to be okay. Mr. Weston seems to have taken a fancy to you. Maybe you'll find out he's not so bad and marry him. Then you won't have to worry about being taken care of, you know?"

Soon, Ella Mae is walking home with Reverend Carter, leaving me there to watch the men throw dirt on my father's coffin. I still have dirt in my hand, squeezing tight.

I can't let it go.

I have to know.

Someone killed my father. And for what?

But the bigger question in my mind and weighing on my heart is... by who? I need proof to put the gambler behind bars and stop this marrying nonsense. But I'm not a fool, either. I can't deny my attraction to the man. Any warm-blooded female with eyes wouldn't be able to look away from the gambler and his fancy duds. It's the eyes, the appeal, and I know deep down he's all for show.

Little by little, I let the dirt drop from my hand. "I'm going to find who did this."

Overhead, the sky rumbles in agreement. The darkness comes rolling in and I am not afraid of a few raindrops. As they grace my hair and my face, I consider who else would want Earl dead. I spoke to Amaryllis. Buck is back at the Triple D, and I can't flee town, so that leaves Warner at the hotel. Maybe I should reconsider the gambler's offer for dinner and get to know him better.

There is a rattle in my chest, and it sounds a lot like thunder. The storm is coming down from the mountain with a vengeance. The air is thick and pungent, and the rain smells of dirty laundry.

Getting soaking wet, and all I can think about is I don't even have the money to buy a headstone.

Another rumble comes from the sky. This time it opens, and the rain pours down.

The men shoveling shout they'll finish later and disappear.

With the rain pouring down, I head for the hotel. By the time I get there, I look like a drowned rat. A woman with a burgundy hat and matching umbrella steps off the stage. Another man in a fancy suit keeps his hat tilted to avoid the rain as he helps her off. Not far behind her an overweight gentleman, with pinstripe pants and a long curly mustache, follows. Half his head is devoid of hair.

"You there, fetch my bag." She points around as if trying to figure out where it is.

"I've got it, ma'am." The bounty hunter has her bag. He's quite the gentleman, opening the door for her. Inside, the bounty hunter leaves the woman's bag at the counter. The clerk greets the men with her, and one of them inquiries about rooms.

The woman's got her hand on the bounty hunter's chest and fluttering her long lashes at him. Why I ought to...

My blood boils at the sight.

Then I hear raised voices from the stairs. Moving a little closer, I spot Amaryllis coming down the stairs with Pierce Weston, a.k.a. The Gambler. Her eyes narrow, and she lets him have it about something, until he catches sight of me and nods in my direction.

Amaryllis pauses, looks at me, then says, "You owe me!" She marches the rest of the way down the stairs. "Good luck with that one." She waves her hand up at the gambler as she goes by me.

He reaches behind his neck and tries to smile away whatever that was. Like his smile could distract me. "Jolene, darlin'. Where have you been? I was looking for you."

I try not to snort. "My father's funeral was today." Some son-in-law he is going to make. What kind of man doesn't show up at his future wife's father's funeral? *The guilty kind,* my thoughts whisper.

"That was today. I'm sorry I wasn't there. Believe me, I would have been, but business ran long and the rain. I was on my way to check on you."

"Drag you to the chapel, more like," comes a mutter from behind. The bounty hunter catches my gaze.

"I'm not insensitive to the death of my bride's father." The gambler puts his arm around me. "We'll marry in the morning, spend the night here at the hotel, then take the stage to Brisbee. I've got some business there before we head out to that claim of ours." He winks.

"Good luck with that." The bounty hunter is off, and I shrug out of the gambler's hold.

"I had hoped we could spend some time together later," I say.

"Sure thing, darlin'. Why don't you run along to that boarding house of yours to freshen up a bit and I'll meet you in the dining room here at the hotel? We can have tea and stay dry from the rain." His smile wavers, and those adorable dimples disappear as his eyes take in my soggy clothes and my hair dripping with rain.

"Fine. I'll meet you back here in an hour."

The overweight gentleman walks around me. He nods to the gambler and doesn't give me a second look.

"You would be wise to dress for supper. The hotel frowns upon riff-raff coming in off the street. They have a certain decorum in which they like to uphold," says a woman.

I turn to find the bounty hunter and the classy woman on his arm. "Oh, Mr. Townes, you are a fine man indeed, to have a heart for those less fortunate. You know, the café down the street might better suitable for someone like yourself," she says, speaking to me again.

She's pretty, with dark hair twisted up in that hat and curls by her face. Her eyes are so blue they're almost purple, and she's petite. Even the gambler can't resist introducing himself.

While they all seem to get to know one another, I learn the woman's name is Daphne Davenport. She holds her gloved hand out for the gambler to kiss.

I leave the men to their new acquaintance and head back out of the hotel. I have half a mind to find Amaryllis first and ask about that argument she had with the gambler, but I don't have to head to the saloon to find her. Soon, I spot her inside Grace's dress shop.

"Can I help you?" Grace hasn't gotten over the remark at church about my dress coming from her shop. I'm sure it did. Although, it wasn't intended for me.

"I thought I spotted Amaryllis."

Grace has an apron on over her white blouse and black skirt. She presses her thin lips together and crosses her arms.

Amaryllis must have stepped behind a screen to try on a dress. I sigh. "May I come in?"

"Paying customers only," she says.

I glance to the window, notice the navy dress missing and, without a penny to my name, I turn away. I go to offer an apology for the misunderstanding after church, but Grace is gone and the door to her store slams shut.

Inside the boarding house, I spot Ruby, who waves me to the kitchen. "I'm sorry again about your father, Jo. I would have come, but I had laundry about to get caught up in the storm. Don't mind the long underwear hanging from the banisters. I put a rope across in the washroom, too. I'm going to need your help with supper tonight, so be back here at four o'clock."

"Of course."

Ruby keeps an orderly kitchen. She has a few regular boarders throughout the week, and a ton on the weekends. I see the sack of potatoes by the door and the vegetables laid on the counter. I'm not shy about peeling a few spuds or getting my hands dirty, but my time is wasting if I want to keep in the company of the gambler and glean any information from him, or a confession.

"Be sure to hang up your wet things. You'll catch your death running around like that." Ruby returns to her household duties, and I head for the stairs.

The last thing I want to do is catch my death. On the other

hand, I think I'd rather get caught dead than in that pink dress of Mary Sue's. The sisters ache in agreement, not wanting to be put in a compromising position again.

On my bed lies a package, wrapped in brown paper, and tied with string. Inside is the navy travel dress with jacket.

Obviously, someone delivered it to the wrong room.

7

There is a constant chill in the air since my father's burial. The rain froze in the night. A mist clings to the air and a damp drizzle comes with the drifting of the clouds.

Last evening, I spent an entire hour in the gambler's company. He taught me to play poker, but I beat him in blackjack. My father liked to play card games on the days the weather shut us in for the winter. We'd drink black coffee and bet with biscuits.

I know it's not really something a girl should do. I doubt Reverend Carter would approve, but sometimes we played rummy. I'm good at rummy and slap jack. The gambler has the upper hand on me when it comes to poker. Twice, I attempted to check out the edge of his coat sleeve. Twice, he took it as me making a pass at him. The third time, he switched it up on me by taking my hand and staring into my eyes. My heart almost jumped out of my chest. His eyes alone are a dangerous prize.

By the end of our afternoon together, he removed his jacket and rolled up his sleeves to deal. No hidden cards there.

I don't believe for a moment the man doesn't carry a gun on him.

I am going to have to up the ante to figure out how to prove he killed my father. The entire rest of the evening, I peeled potatoes for Ruby and hinted about the package on my bed.

If the gambler was disappointed, he said not a word. Even when Ms. Davenport and an overweight gentleman came into the dining hall later, the gambler kept his eyes on me.

He walked me back to the boarding house and held both my hands. "The preacher had to make some visits to folks outside of town and said he could marry us Wednesday morning. I'll come calling tomorrow evening for dinner again."

Oh Lord, those eyes of his were killer.

My reservations almost cracked a little and part of me wants to believe he is innocent, and I should take the leap and marry him. But there is something to be said about the way he walks and how carefully he speaks. Most of that afternoon, while we played cards, all he wanted to discuss was me, my father's mine, and how he was the luckiest man alive.

Or the deadliest.

I know no more about Pierce Weston, the gambler, than I did on the day he won my hand in marriage in a card game. However, I learned the man came from down south and rode a steamboat on the Mississippi during a weeklong card tournament.

His accent isn't from the south. It sounds more eastern, and to the north. I met some black folks in the mountains when I was younger. Their accents were thicker and held a longer drawl compared to the gambler. Although by the time he left me at Ruby's door, he claimed New Orleans was originally where he was born.

He'd come a long way to be here.

Instead of gold or silver shimmering in his eyes, like most

men out to find their fortunes, all I see in his eyes is the reflection of dollar signs.

I don't see the bounty hunter in the morning as I help Ruby clear away the breakfast dishes. I've got washing duty, and she's on the drying side.

"You hear anything from the sheriff?"

My hands are wrist deep in dishwater. "Nope."

"I can't say I'm surprised. Many people could have shot your father. Most did not like Earl. He had a way of rubbing them the wrong way. Never knew when to keep his mouth shut." Ruby towel dries a plate and puts it on the clean pile.

"He could be downright mean after drinking too much firewater. Sometimes I wonder if that's why my mother took off. He used to keep a photo of her. I've got it now. I should have buried it with him."

I've looked at that photo a hundred times in the last few days. I tell Ruby Chord, the bounty hunter, delivered the photo and my face turns hot thinking about referring to him by first name.

Ruby gets this dreamy gaze and sighs. "He's a good man, Chord Townes. It's a shame life jilted him."

"What do you mean?" I hand her another wet plate.

"No business of mine to tell." She dries the last plate and changes the subject. "Have you talked to the Swanson sisters? Maybe one of them know something. Your father would have gone there before the saloon, or maybe after? He would have wanted to get all cleaned up for his daughter's wedding."

I give her a look and we both laugh. Earl? Clean up for my wedding? There's a thought. She might not be far off from thinking he would have gone there. The three places my father always visited in town were the bathhouse, the saloon, and the claims office.

"Or how about the barber?"

I shake my head. "I do the sheering and the shaving. Earl

wouldn't have paid someone to chop at his mop or his chin. He liked his beard." I shove away the memories floating up and try to swallow down the lump in my throat.

Mean, ornery goat. Don't know why I miss him.

"You should talk to Emma or Eva." Ruby dries her hands on her apron. "Right after you take a bath of your own and try on that dress on your bed. I was the one who was here when Robbie delivered it. I figured it came from Grace's. That gambling man isn't wasting any expense on you."

"Then I suppose he won't mind paying for me to take a bath now, will he?"

Ruby catches my drift and grins. There is one way for a person to get inside the Swanson sisters' place, and I'm feeling downright dirty.

"You better watch your step, Jo. You're going to end up the talk of the town."

After the pink dress appearance at church, I'm afraid I already am. Maybe a few stains to my reputation will send the gambling man running in the opposite direction.

After all, there is always Daphne Davenport for him to go courting. She'd be better suited for him and his fancy duds than a plain Jane like me.

I glance down at my dusty pants and muddy boots. I'm far from fetching and I've been wearing my hair in this style since age nine.

I bite my lip and contemplate.

What do I have to lose?

It's not like I *want* to marry the gambler. Do I?

No lady in her respectable manner would ever go traipsing into the Swanson Bathhouse. It's a regal-looking mansion on the upper end of town. It's said to have belonged to the original settler in this valley. At one point, it belonged to Jeremiah Redwood, the first mayor of town. The old Redwood estate soon got swallowed up as part of the town when new settlers came to claim their parcels in search of their fortunes. Old Redwood died, leaving no kin behind, and Redwood soon became Deadwood. The man never took a wife in fear he might one day have to share his estate. Legend had it, it ended up in the hands of a far relative and later passed on to old man Swanson, the twins' father. No one has seen Emma and Eve's daddy in a decade, but the sisters still swear he's alive in the house.

As many men frequent the establishment, no one dares contest his existence.

Boy, do I feel dirty stepping inside.

The place is sparkling with white columns and a second-story balcony. The front porch runs the entire length of the house, where a few rockers sit in front of the tall windows. Black shutters hang beside the windows, far taller than I.

The foyer is grander than the Warner Hotel. An open sweeping staircase greets me. From down the hall, a woman wrapped in a shawl looking like she rolled straight from bed pauses at the sight of me.

Her voice is husky from sleep. "You looking for someone?"

"I'm looking for a bath."

Her eyes are smokey, smeared from sleeping with kohl around her eyes. She turns her head and shouts, "Eva!"

The shorter of the two sisters comes to the top of the stairs. Her hair hangs down, long and draping over her shoulders. She's dressed primly in a button-down blouse and a skirt that slims her. The bustle is pinned up in the back, and she slowly makes her way down the staircase towards me. Her hand glides over the polished banister.

"You're not at all what I thought you would be from afar. Turn around." She twirls her fingers and I oblige. "You're one of those folks from up in the mining claims, aren't you? I can't say I blame you for wanting to escape. I suppose you might do."

Eva presses out her lips. She steps down from the last step and places her hand on my shoulder. "You look familiar. Do I know you?"

"I was hoping you might remember my father."

"If you've come here looking to peek in my rooms to find him, I have to tell you, I have a strict policy of confidentiality of my customers."

"My father's dead." It comes out softly, as a whisper.

"I see." Eva glances down the hall where the previous woman reappears with a slightly taller version of Eva's twin. Emma holds her head high, her dark hair piled on top of her head. "Emma, we've got ourselves a lost one."

Emma presses her hand to her heart. "Do we now?"

"Did either of you know my father? He might have come here before he died."

"Was it recent?" Emma asks, lifting a brow.

"Saturday night. Earl Dean. He comes here every time we visit town."

Eva taps her finger over her mouth.

Emma nods, staring off in the distance, then shrugs. "A lot of men come here to get cleaned up before going out for a night on the town." She winks. "We can't remember them all. Policy."

Eva shakes her head. "I knew him. Complained about paying extra for a back scrub. As if soap were free." She clucks. "Just what happened to him?"

"Somebody shot him."

Eva frowns. "Oh, that's dirty."

Emma crosses her arms, stepping back to take a long, hard look at me. "I take it you got nowhere else to go? No other kin? No husband?"

The way she says husband makes my insides roll.

"Come now, poor girl lost her father," Eva chides. "Knowing them prospectors, she probably doesn't have a dime to her name. It isn't her fault she's been cooped up in those mountains for so long she doesn't have a husband."

"Well, we could take her. Tilly ran off last week, and we could use a maid." Emma waves her hand.

"Or we could send her to Edith. She'll have her matched up with a man in no time."

"Oh, I don't need a man. I have a man. I mean, there's one that wants to marry me." I glance around the foyer, thinking this might be a good time to escape. Obviously, these two aren't going to help me find my father's killer.

"Then why are you here, sugar?" Emma asks.

"A bath."

Eva laughs. It's rich and delightful and puts a scowl on Emma's face. Eva leans in close and whispers, "You know you're the first woman who has had the nerve to come here for *that*."

Emma coughs and Eva belts her one on the back.

"Really, ladies. I came for a bath." I hold out my arms. I tell them about the gambler, my father's last bet, and the dress awaiting me on the bed.

"If you're staying at the boarding house, old Ruby's got a tub," Emma says in her Southern drawl.

"I'll have to drag it into the kitchen, and I'm not about to do that with all her other boarders," I'm quick to make up an excuse.

"Well, then," Eva says when Emma interrupts. "Who did you say wanted to marry you?"

"Pierce Weston."

Eva's eyes light up along with Emma's and the two sisters get identical sly smiles on their lips.

"Did you hear that, Eva?" Emma says. "She's Mr. Weston's bride."

"I think we can arrange for a bath." Eva shakes her bustle and winks. "And don't you worry, we'll charge your soon-to-be husband." She claps her hands. "Minnie! Prepare a bath in the private room on the east wing."

I hope Mr. Weston's got deep pockets in those pinstripe trousers he likes to wear.

As we go up the stairs, I ask, "My father wouldn't have by chance left a boot here when he left?"

"Men leave a lot of things here. They usually always come back for their boots." Emma takes off down the hall.

"Not both, just one," I clarify.

"One?" Eva holds up a finger.

"He was missing a boot."

"You won't find it here."

As we reach the top of the stairs, a door swings open and a curvy brunette slips out. Inside, I glimpse long hair, a square jaw, and naked shoulders. His head turns and gray eyes the color of the recent storm widen with recognition. I duck my head and hurry along.

What's it any of my business if the bounty hunter is having a private bath? I know for a fact there's a community room downstairs. My father wouldn't have afforded a private bath like the ones upstairs.

Is it getting hot in here?

I follow Emma to the other end of the hall. Inside, I get the full spa treatment. Two women prepare my bath—hot, steaming water and lots of suds. Eva brings me bath salts and a cube of jasmine smelling soap. "You're going to have to take off your clothes if you want to bathe."

It's a porcelain tub, one of those fancy ones from back east. "Don't be shy now, just us girls."

I look down at the sisters. I haven't ever shown them to

anyone. Well, not on purpose. I have a sneaking suspicion Chitto might have spied on me a time or two.

Eva snaps her fingers at me. I grab the linen and start stripping behind it. Wrapped in the fabric, I go to the tub. Minnie grabs the fabric and I slide down below the suds.

Eva departs and leaves me in Minnie's hands.

By the time I'm through, my skin glows a gentle hue of pink and my hair has never been this clean. Minnie, a petite girl with olive-colored skin, sets to untangling my wild mane. She's none too gentle and offers to put it in a fancy braid.

When she's done, I don't recognize the woman staring at the mirror. "You should have your own shop styling hair." I twist my head back and forth. She braided my hair from one side to the other, then twisted it up in the back. It's all held in place by some pins.

"I was a lady's maid back east."

"What brought you west?"

Minnie sighs. "I answered one of those mail-order bride ads."

"So, you're married?"

"Widow. Dumb fool got shot two days after the wedding. Left me nothing but a lame horse and a worn bedroll."

"I'm sorry for your loss." I can't imagine coming all the way out here to end up widowed and working in a bathhouse. It makes me think of the bounty hunter, and for once, I'm a little envious of Minnie and her coworkers.

And I can't believe I let my mind go there. It's no business of mine what goes on in that room. For all I know, the bounty hunter is relaxing and getting the spa treatment, too. Who am I to judge a man for liking a bubble bath?

I've got my own motives for being here. Sure, I could have taken a bath at Ruby's, but not as fancy as this, and I wouldn't have gotten any information from the Swanson sisters. Not that they were all too helpful in that department, anyway.

While I soak and relax in the bubbles, Eva sends one of her girls to the boarding house where Ruby gave her my dress. Shame on me for taking off without it. There is no way Eva would let me leave with a clean body and put on dirty duds.

It's past lunch by the time Minnie helps me figure out all the buttons and clasps to get into the dress.

"Now, that's a sight I never thought I'd see," Eva declares. She snaps her fingers. "Minnie, be a dear and dispose of these filthy clothes."

I rush to grab them, and Eva rolls her eyes. "Now why would you want to keep these when you can look like that?"

And by looking like that, she means like an entirely different woman. I'm all squeezed into the slim skirt with the big bustle in the back. The sisters aren't uncomfortable, but the way this skirt hugs my hips should be outlawed.

The blouse collar goes up my neck, but the jacket is my favorite piece. It fits nicely, and I think I'll wear it all the time.

"Tilly!" Eva screams at the girl who fetched my dress. "You forgot the shoes!"

"Oh, I've got my boots."

Eva goes white. "Boots? You can't wear cowboy boots with a dress like that!"

"What's wrong with my boots?" I glance down at them. There is still a little mud crusted around the soles.

"It's too bad you already have a groom, or Edith over in Cripple Creek would have you instructed on the proper etiquette for a wife."

"I ain't in need of any etiquette." I'm headed back up those mountains to ensure the peace between Tail Feathers and keeping our mine claim from falling into the wrong hands. I don't tell Eva and bite my lip from doing so.

"Ain't isn't a word, missy." Minnie plops a navy hat with netting and a ribbon flower on my head.

"I don't recall that as mine."

"It's from a few seasons ago. Consider it a wedding gift."
Eva laughs and heads for the door. "Well, I'm sure that fancy-
pants husband of yours will make sure you know all you need
to of being a wife. If not, invite me to tea." She grins, sly like
before. "Now you tell Mr. Weston it was the Swanson sisters
that got you all cleaned up and ready for your big day, you
hear?" Her fake Southern charm and accent come out to play.

"Thank you. And I'll be taking my other clothes with me."
I roll them up and follow Eva out.

Going down the stairs is much harder than when I went up.
I keep my clothes rolled under one arm and my other hand
clutching the banister.

The skirt is so restricting, a girl could fall on her face taking
a regular stride. No wonder Eva Swanson thinks I need lessons
on being a lady. I never claimed to be one of those fancy ladies
like back east or even from the south. I'm mountain born and,
in this skirt, there won't be any running for the hills any time
soon.

I nearly trip and fall down the stairs at the sight of the wide
shoulders and long, dark hair belonging to the bounty hunter
standing in the foyer. Emma Swanson has her hand on his
chest, and I swear I can't go anywhere without seeing a female
swoon all over the man. For once, his duster is over his arm,
revealing the gun belt hanging low on his hip and the six-
shooter tied to his thigh.

The man is one lean, mean, gunslinging machine.

My legs would buckle if it wasn't for this darn skirt. I think
I'd rather take my chances with the pink number Ella Mae
gave me once belonging to her sister.

"If there's anything else I can do for you..." Emma runs a
finger down his chest.

The bounty hunter politely moves her hand away. He nods
in my direction. "You clean up nice."

"I could say the same about you." Flares of heat hit my

cheeks, and he tilts his head back, about to laugh. The man is more solid than a rock.

"Don't smile now. It might ruin your reputation," I say.

He laughs, and it makes me bust a smile. I might not have gotten what I wanted from the Swanson sisters, but hearing the deep rumbling sound from Chord Townes vocals makes it all worth it.

He offers me his arm. "May I escort the lady out?"

"Be careful, this one is taken." Emma steps back beside Eva. "See you again soon?"

"Ladies." The bounty hunter puts on his hat, and we head outside to a dry sky.

8

There is no other way to avoid getting the edge of my skirt
dirty than to hike it up a bit and show off my cowboy boots.
The bounty hunter is a gentleman. "Nice boots."

"Thank you." I doubt he meant it as a compliment. While
he doesn't go throwing his duster across the way for me to walk
on, he keeps his arm at my disposal as we cross the street.

"So, you decided to marry the suit."

"What makes you say that?"

His face is chiseled perfection. His lips press in, and I
wonder what it would be like to have lips like his kiss a girl.
They'd pack quite a wallop, I imagine. Not that I want to find
out. Okay, maybe I do, but obviously, the bounty hunter
doesn't see me that way. I surmise he's not married, otherwise
he better hope his wife doesn't find out he had a private bath at
the Swanson Bathhouse.

"You don't seem the type." We reach the plank boardwalk
under the local diner. I bristle a little at his remark.

"Type?" Because I was at the bathhouse. I open my mouth
to give him a good piece of my mind and drop the hold on my
skirt.

He holds up his free hand. "You look uncomfortable, Dimples."

I am. I take two steps and forget I can't stretch to my regular stride. I tip forward and heaven be, the man catches me for the second time since we've met. "It's the bustle in the back," I say. "It throws a girl off balance."

There's not a wrinkle by his eye showing he believes me. "Then don't wear it."

I've still got my other clothes tucked under my arm. They could use a good laundering.

"You don't mind a woman wearing pants?" I ask.

"I'm not easily intimidated like other men." The bounty hunter stops. His eyes hood as he looks at me. My heart does this pitter patter, and I'm sure he's sent many a woman swooning with those sinful eyes of his. There's an invisible lasso between us, slowly roping us in, closer and closer.

He reaches behind him, opens the door, and holds it for me.

I take a moment to get my bearings and realize we are at the sheriff's office. I go inside to find Sheriff Bently drinking coffee and finishing a piece of upside-down cake from the diner we passed.

"Chord." He nods. "And who might this be?"

I reach up and touch my hair. Did a bath, new clothes, and a hairdo change me so much the man can't recognize me?

"Jo Dean," I tell him. "My father was the one shot behind the saloon."

His eyes bulge, and he chokes on his cake.

Chord, I mean Mr. Townes—you know, the bounty hunter —twitches his lips as we watch the sheriff straighten in his seat.

"You'll have to forgive me. You look different from when I saw you last."

I reach up again to pat my hair, a habit I soon see forming. Not that I can afford to have Minnie do my hair like this every day. I suppose I could take more time with it while I'm in town. My enclosed legs beg to differ from getting around in this dress all day. I do not know how the other ladies in the east manage it, or maybe I need to take some lessons from Daphne Davenport, the ©Eastern belle from off the stagecoach.

"Nothing to forgive."

"I suppose you got your father's claim all squared away. I feared we'd have more trouble over it in the coming of days. Your husband is a mighty lucky fellow."

"Oh, I'm not married." Yet. "I wanted to check on how the investigation was going to find my father's killer. You have enough evidence to put away the gambler for cheating my father and killing him, don't you?"

I hear wedding bells chiming in the back of my mind and wince.

"Deadwood is a town filled with murderers and thieves. I don't have enough manpower to track down every killer. Sure, I do my best, but sometimes in cases like this, you never know who done it. Your father had a lot to lose and a lot of people who were after it."

"Are you saying you're not going to keep looking for the killer? I told you, I know it was the gambler. He cheated and coerced my father into losing the deed to our claim."

"And throw you in the pot to boot." Sheriff Bently leans forward on his elbows. "I've talked to Buck out at the Triple D, and I've talked to Jed Warner over at the hotel. No one held a gun to your father and made him put his claim in the pot. He threw you in for good measure." He shook his head. "I'm sorry, but you are of age, you could go to the judge when he comes in town next Tuesday to refute it, but in cases like this, you are better off getting married, enjoying a life of ease with all that money, and forgetting about the killer."

"Marry the gambler? Have you forgotten he's the one who could have murdered my father? You can't let him get away with this! You're the law! What about justice? You have to arrest him."

The bounty hunter rests his hand on my arm and the shock of his touch pulls me back from slugging the sheriff. My insides are on fire and my fingers clench in a fist. The bundle of clothes under my arm is on the floor.

"Easy, Dimples. The sheriff is right. There is no evidence against Weston other than cheating."

"Ha!" I yell. "You admit he cheated!"

"There might be a witness who will testify he did, but it doesn't prove he killed anyone." Sheriff Bently scratches the back of his thick neck.

"Amaryllis." I *knew* she knew something.

"I can't reveal the names of my sources."

"And you can't find my father's killer. What good are you?" I spew.

"Dimples," the bounty hunter warns.

"Don't you Dimples me." I whirl around on him, gritting my teeth as this atrocious skirt tightens around me as I swivel. "You're not being forced to get married or about to lose your home and your life."

A little muscle in the side of his jaw ticks. Those gray eyes cloud, paler than before, and I bite back against letting any more words out. There's a pain in his expression. Then he blinks, and it's gone. "No one is forcing you to marry anyone." The bounty hunter looks at the sheriff.

Bently raises his shoulders. "It's rough country, little lady. We have a code here in the west. Your father tossed your hand in marriage in the pot, you're expected to honor it."

"Honor it?" I choke back the injustice of it all.

"Well, I suppose if you haven't gotten married, would it be safe for me to assume with the way you're dressed, you're on your way to meet your future husband?"

"No," both me and the bounty hunter say at the same time.

"I'm not marrying anyone until my father's killer is brought to justice."

"Chord?" Sheriff Bentely looks at the bounty hunter.

"I'm headed out of town on another bounty."

He must have gotten the rest of his bounty money. It makes sense. The man got a bath and all cleaned up. He's hitting the trail again on another mission to track down a notorious outlaw for the reward. But there is a murderer running loose right here in Deadwood.

"You can't leave. You have to catch my father's killer." My chest feels tight. It's getting harder to breathe, and I press my hand against my chest. The sisters are heaving while my lungs are squeezing for air.

"Sheriff Bentely has it under control. I don't go solving crimes, Dimples. I know who I'm after and I go get them."

"He's all but said he's giving up," I cry.

"Not giving up, just letting you know there's a chance I won't find who did this right away," Sheriff Bentely says. *If ever.* I can see it written across his face, plain as day.

"Did you find the boot?" I ask.

"The boot?" Sheriff Bentely frowns.

"My father's missing boot. Someone stole the boot off his foot after he died."

Both the sheriff and the bounty hunter exchange a look.

I huff and wave my hands like a madwoman. It's clear they don't think the boot is important. "So does this mean I can leave town and go back to my place?"

Once I tell Tail Feathers and Stands With Two Deer what has happened, they'll send a war party out to take care of the gambler. On second thought, maybe I'll leave the part out about the gambler and let them figure out he's the killer on their own. But I'll have an entire posse to help protect my home and bring justice to my father.

"I'm afraid not. You'll have to wait until the judge comes to settle this marriage business and claim on your property. Besides, I haven't ruled out you may have been the one who killed your father for promising you to Mr. Weston or wanting the claim he holds up in the mountain for yourself."

"It's already half mine," I blurt.

Again, both the sheriff and the bounty hunter exchange a look.

"It's safer if you stay in town."

The bounty hunter gathers up my clothes on the floor, and I snatch them from him.

Outside the sheriff's office, the bounty hunter stares out in the distance. "You want me to put you up on my horse and give you a ride to the church on my way out of town?"

I grab hold of the bounty hunter. "You can't leave. You have to help me."

"I've got a reward poster calling to cash in." He pats his pocket. He's back to wearing his long leather duster. It looks good on him. Maybe too good, for Hannah calls to him and waves. He tips his hat politely never taking his eyes from me.

The gambler strolls out of the diner. Not far behind him is the bank owner Mr. Campbell. I turn away and hope the gambler doesn't spot me.

"I'll pay you. Whatever that reward is." I point to his pocket, desperate.

The bounty hunter goes to step off the walk and I grab onto him and hold tight. "Please. I'll double it."

His eyes level with mine. "That's a big promise and a lot of cash, Dimples. How do I know you'll pay up?"

"I'll give you a percentage of my claim's worth to hold as collateral." It's the last thing I have left. Plus, I'm going to have to find a job while in town. I have a feeling my stay will keep getting extended longer and longer.

The bounty hunter steps back up on the walk. "Who else have you made that offer to?"

"Just you."

His eyes get that hooded, sultry look again. It opens a pot stove of heat in my belly.

"I'll help you on two conditions." He leans in. "One, you don't make that offer to anyone else but me."

I lick my lips, the heat bisecting my belly. "Second?"

"You hold off on any matrimonial plans until after we've settled."

It's hard to judge a man's intention when he looks at you as if you're his only meal of the day.

"I've got one condition of my own," I pant.

"Who said this was a negotiation, Dimples?" His voice rumbles, and my hand is right back on his arm.

"I can't leave town, but you can." This is a bad idea. A terrible idea, but what else is a girl to do?

"I'm not sneaking you out of town."

"There are some families in the mountains waiting on supplies. They'll get angry if they don't get them soon." It's half the truth. I don't mention they're native descent and they may or may not be living off the reservation.

"I'm not a delivery boy," he says.

"You deliver bodies," I counter.

The bounty hunter isn't one to smile easily. He tilts his head back. "There is only one body I'm interested in at the moment."

I'm on fire everywhere thanks to this man.

"Let's step back inside the sheriff's office, Dimples. I want it in writing before I go tracking down a killer."

And just like that, it's a done deal.

When I come back outside, the gambler is waiting for me with a smile as wide as the whole Dakota Territory.

Those sparkling green emeralds in his eyes tell me he's up to no good. I keep the promissory note tucked away from sight. I'll have to file it with the claims department another day.

For now, there is something wicked in the gambler's gaze. I'm in over my head and getting deeper in trouble by the minute.

I leave my rolled-up clothes with Sherman, the clerk, at the hotel desk. Inside the dining room, Miss Daphne Davenport stands beside the portly fellow, whom I am introduced to as her father, David Davenport. Beside him is a tall gentleman with a wily mustache by the name of Thomas Conway. He looks down his nose at me as the gambler places his hand on my back and pushes me into their little group.

Daphne has her hair twisted and in curls. Her pink lips turn up in a smile in the gambler's presence. Before I know it, he leaves me to get us drinks and Daphne is leaning in towards me. "Your husband is a fine gentleman. It's too bad our stage got delayed in Silver Valley. Rumor has it he won you in a card game."

"An unfortunate event," I say, my eyes on the gambler's back. He must feel my eyes boring into his shoulder blades. He turns his head and winks my way. Daphne's eyes widen and she places her gloved hand over her lips and giggles. "Oh, you are a lucky woman."

"I hardly call it luck."

Daphne reaches up to fix her hair as Jed Warner comes into the hotel's lounge. He's tugging on his tie and heading our way.

"Daddy says this town is lucky for the railroad coming through. If it wasn't for him and Thomas." Her cheeks pinken at the faux pas of calling Mr. Conway by his first name. "Mr. Conway and Daddy are connecting the east to the west. Why, with all that new abundant wealth and your husband, you'll be able to travel back east." Her attention is no longer on me but divided between the hotel's owner and my gambling man.

Well, not *my* gambling man. He's not even my husband.

"You'll love it back east," she continues. "Daddy says I can take the train back any time I want. You won't have to wait for the latest fashion." Then she points to my bustle skirt. "I hadn't realized how long it took things to reach the west. Thomas—Mr. Conway —was right to talk Daddy into investing in the railroad. And as soon as they bust right through the mountain, we won't have to wait for last season's fashion to arrive. I will be on the same timeline as all of my friends back east."

The gambler arrives with offerings of wine. Daphne is the first to accept. I take the glass from his hand. The gambler's fingers brush against mine, and a bloom of heat bursts in my belly. Husband. Mountain. Railroad.

I take a deep gulp of red wine and try to smile as Mr. Davenport and Mr. Conway turn their conversation our way. Mr. Conway hasn't stopped looking at me, or maybe it's Daphne the man can't take his eyes off. Nope, it's me. He's looking at me, and those hollowed eyes of his put a chill in my bones. I step closer to the gambler on reflex.

"Weston, I see you found your beautiful wife to join us." Mr. Davenport holds out his hand. I give him my free one, and the man lifts it to his mouth and kisses the top. He's laying it on thick, those fat lips of his pressing hard against my skin. I snap my hand back quick.

"My wife is not accustomed to other men handling her." The gambler grins and Davenport, along with Conway, match his expression.

"No worries, my dear." Davenport waves it off. "My Daphne here will be happy to help you fit back into society. It must be a great relief to you after spending so much time up in the mountains away from civilization."

"Is it true what they say?" Daphne asks. "Are there really Indians up in those mountains?"

Jed Warner steps into our little conversation by saying, "Don't you worry, Miss Davenport," Jed Warner says, stepping into our little conversation. "The only natives around here are the miners. The Indians are all on a reservation."

"But isn't there one here in the territory?" Daphne's eyes round out, and I can tell she has got all the men's undying attention.

"Don't you worry." Warner worms his way closer to Daphne. "They leave the reservation, and the army will put them right back."

"What about rogues?" Conway asks.

The gambler slips his hand around my waist. It's nice, but my mind is on Stands With Two Deer and Tail Feathers. Standing Rock is close to our land claim in the mountains. If the army finds them, well, I don't want to think about what will happen to all those precious people.

"No Indian would dare try to come down into town. A fine woman of your status has no worries," Warner assures her.

If only I had the same reassurance. "Mr. Conway." I cringe at having to address my attention toward him, but I must know. "I'm told you're bringing the railroad to Deadwood. You're coming through the mountain?"

Beside me, the gambler stiffens.

"Why yes, I am. We've got track going down outside of Silver Valley and headed this way," Mr. Conway confirms.

"Soon we'll have a rail running through the entire Black Hills." Mr. Davenport hooks his thumbs in his vest pockets and boasts out his wide girth. He's a pleasant sort of man, with a plump face and turning a little bald on top.

The entire Black Hills. The wine in my mouth turns sour. What will happen to the people at Standing Rock?

"Your husband is about to become a very wealthy man.

That must please you." Mr. Conway glances around. He holds his finger up and catches the attention of one of the hotel staff.

"He's not my husband," I blurt.

Davenport and Conway exchange a glance. Daphne chatters away with Warner.

The gambler dismisses my outburst. "Technicality, I assure you. We'll be married by morning. Isn't that right, darlin'?"

"Not until we find my father's killer," I inform them all.

"Well, that is unfortunate." Mr. Davenport looks at the gambler.

"I assure you, gentlemen, this will not affect our deal. The judge will be here on Tuesday." The gambler is sweating. Come to think of it, I believe it's getting too stuffy in here for me. Or perhaps it's the dress. I'm tempted to ask Daphne to borrow the fan hanging from her wrist.

"Deal?"

"For the land." Mr. Conway pauses for a moment, ordering a drink.

I look at the gambler. "What land?"

"Why our land, darlin,"

I've got a drop of wine left in my glass. I swirl it as things click together in my mind.

"You mean my land? My father's land?"

"The land that's now mine. Ours." He hitches an eyebrow. He doesn't want me to make a scene. I take a deep breath. There is no way I am letting him get away with this.

"You're a no good swindler," I seethe in a low whisper.

"And look what it got me." He leans in. "You're a treasure, Jolene Dean. I can't wait to make you my wife."

"Why wait?" Davenport moves and comes between Warner and his daughter. Warner frowns but steps aside like a gentleman. He must have seen him getting too close. I feel the same way about the gambler. He tightens his hold around my waist.

"We could have a wedding dinner right here at the hotel."

I glare at Warner.

Daphne's lips turn into a pout. I'd gladly trade places with her. It's obvious she's pining after my man. Gah! I have to stop thinking of him in this manner.

"No." I put my foot down, a little harder than I intend, as it causes the gambler to jump back and scowl at me.

"Now, Jolene, darlin'—"

"Don't you Jolene me." I shove the wineglass in his hands, and he winces, still trying to find his footing. "It's Jo, and I've got a killer to find." I march off, stumble, and am about to trip when the gambler reaches from behind to steady me. I leave out a huff and say to them all. "Stay off my land."

"That's my land, too."

"We'll see about that." I hike up my skirt, not caring if I'm showing my boot covered calves. Daphne gasps and slaps her hand over her lips at the sight of them.

I make my way right out of the hotel. "Does that mean we're not having dinner?" Daphne's voice floats out the hotel along with me. Sherman's at the counter, looking a bit startled. A stray hair sticks straight up in the back of his head. Poor guy.

Now, more so than ever, I'm convinced the gambler shot my father.

9

The day has almost gotten away from me, and I've made it nowhere. The sun is a dark gold in the distance. Beneath it lies the mountains and my heart aches for home. I have half a mind to go back and talk to the sheriff again, maybe convince him to let me leave town, and call off the bounty hunter. If I can escape into the mountains, then I can hide from the gambler, but it won't fix the mess my father has gotten me into. I should go jump on his grave and yell at him in the heavens, but I won't waste the energy on that no-good corpse of his.

Halfway down the walk, a hand reaches out and grabs my shoulder. Every fiber in my body goes on alert. I take that hand and twist. As I turn, the man yowls and I come face to face with a very shocked and wilting Sherman. His knees buckle as I twist his arm up and he's almost bowing down to me.

"Y-you forgot y-your clo-clothes…"

My heart hammers, but I release him. He holds out the rolled-up garments in his good hand, then he scampers back. He flops his arm I twisted and wince. "No woman should be that strong."

I laugh and watch as he hurries back to the hotel. As I turn, another hand reaches around me, covers my mouth, and drags me from the planked walk. I struggle and try to scream, but soon I'm behind the barbershop. When the hand releases me, I whirl around, shove my clothes in front of me like a weapon, and stop.

Chitto stands before me, his eyebrows drawn together, a deep frown on his face, and that hawk-like nose of his pointed up in indigitation.

I lower the clothes, not that my pants would do me any good, although I'd sure get around easier in them.

"What are you doing here?" I hiss at him. Wildly, I look around, hoping no one has spotted him.

He draws me over behind the barbershop, away from the back door, and presses me against the wood siding. "Tail Feathers sent me. You take too long this time. Why haven't you returned?"

There is concern in his voice and a little possessiveness. His fingers grip over my arm as he takes in my attire. "You are becoming more like them."

I ignore his comment. "My father is dead. The sheriff won't let me leave town. You need to go. You shouldn't be here."

He tilts his head back, those dark eyes of his giving me a piercing look. They're filled with sorrow, with shock, and I dare say the light of lust. I'm not his. Not then. Not now. And he's got a woman back in the mountains whose name isn't mine.

"Tail Feathers is without tobacco. Your father promised. He will not be pleased."

"I'm working on it. I'll keep my father's promise, but you need to get out of here before someone sees you."

Chitto shakes his head. "I leave when you leave. I will not leave you here without a man to protect you."

I roll my eyes. Part of me is happy to have him say it. The other makes me wince. "I'm plenty protected. I've got Shorty."

That's what my father called his sawed-off shotgun I have hidden in my bed at Ruby's place. "And I've got two men who have a stake in finding my father's killer. They won't let nothing happen to me."

What I said to reassure Chitto darkens his expression. "Two men? There should be no men. I am your husband."

"No," I tell him firmly. "You're not."

"You still have my ponies."

"You can take them back. They're in the stables with the blacksmith."

He lifts his head as sound comes down the alley and we both tense.

"You need to leave," I whisper. "I'm sending supplies. As soon as things are settled here, I'm coming back."

His chest puffs. "Then I will provide for you. I will be your husband in all ways."

I shake my head. "Not by the laws of my people." *Not in a million years,* I think. Sure, when we were young, the kisses were nice, and I might have been miffed at Earl for not letting Chitto take me to his sleeping mat, but I'm a wiser woman, more mature. And this close to Chitto doesn't put the fires in my belly like they do when the bounty hunter gives me that hooded look, nor like when the gambler flirts.

"Your people have been scouting along the mountains. They have camped near our claim."

I don't bother arguing about there is no "our" in his statement. No, my heart speeds up faster than a galloping horse. Now it's my turn to grip him. "Who are they? Have they spotted you?"

"There are many in the distance. Do not worry, we will ensure no one tries squatting on the land, but Tail Feathers will not hold them off or put our tribe in danger unless your father's deal is paid," he says.

To do so would mean revealing themselves and they

would get in trouble for being off the reservation. The last thing I want is the Calvary marching in and pushing them back into the invisible corral where they've been forced to live.

"I'm sending a man with Tail Feathers' payment. I will have him leave it at the opening of the mine."

"This man... who is he?"

"A friend." I have no other way to describe him. "His name is Chord Townes."

"I have heard of this Townes. He hunts men for money. What makes you think he would not turn us in to the army?"

"Because he has a bigger stake at risk." Or I hope. I hadn't thought this plan through enough. A few renegade Indians were the least of my problems.

"Three days." Chitto leans and touches his forehead to mine. "I do not think we can keep the squatters from entering the land for long. They come and camp on the other side of the gulch. There is talk of the great iron road."

"I know."

The back door of the barbershop opens. Chitto whirls around and I do my best to hide him. Hung Lai Woh steps out, a bucket of hair in his hand. I try not to curl my nose up. He nods, peering around me for a moment. He goes about his business of dumping the hair and gives me another look. "Woman should not stay back here alone."

He goes back inside. I turn and Stands With Two Deer is gone. To me, he'll always be Chitto, but husband material he is not. Besides, I've got more important things to worry about besides tobacco.

Three days.

The iron road is coming.

I'm sure my father's murder has everything to do with it, as do my impending nuptials to the gambler. If he thinks for a moment he can bluff me, I'll be one step ahead of him. I am convinced more than ever the gambler is guilty. Who else would stand to profit from my father's death?

It's no coincidence the railroad gurus are in town.

They're after my father's land. I've got a surprise for them. Over *my* dead body were they going to get it.

First thing the next morning, I head to the dress shop. I'm back in my britches, and I've got my hat tilted low to keep the glare of the morning sun from blinding me.

Last night, I hardly slept a wink thanks to Chitto, the bounty hunter, and the gambler. I reached for Shorty twice when there was a creak in front of my door. I miss the tiny cabin in the mountains and the sounds of the birds in the morning. Instead, the shouts of men from across the road and the ping of a hammer from down at the stables fill the air. I'm half tempted to stop in and check on those ponies and a particularly muscle-armed blacksmith, but I have got a dress to contend with and a murderer to find.

I agreed to meet the bounty hunter later at the mercantile. I swallow down the butterflies hatching and swirling inside me at the thought.

The bell chimes above the door as I enter Grace's dress shop. She takes one look at me and the dress box in my hands and says, "Well, if you're looking for me to alter this one so it fits better than the last, you'll have to get in line, and you'll have to wait until that husband-to-be of yours pays his bill."

Grace pulls out another pin and Amaryllis sucks in a breath. "Ow. Go easy, will you?" Her curly locks brush across her shoulder as she looks back at me. "I heard about the dress fiasco."

"Not my fault. The man insisted he had to have that dress

for his bride." Grace says before putting a pin in her mouth and shrugs.

"Well, as soon as Grace gets done pinning me like a rag doll, we can head to my closet. I'm sure I've got something in there that might suit better for a night with Mr. Fancy Pants." She wiggled her shoulders.

Grace stuck her with another pin and Amaryllis yowls like an old alley cat. "Just because you haven't got a man, Grace, doesn't mean you have to go sticking it to us who do."

Grace laughs and shakes her head. She backs away from Amaryllis. She's a beautiful woman with high cheekbones and soft eyes. The shop once belonged to her mother, who took over after her father passed. It was a tailor shop, then a widow's way of keeping an income. Grace took over the shop, and I can't help wondering why no cowboy has taken over her heart. Although rumor once had it she'd fallen in love with a silver-smith who took off for greener pastures, leaving Grace behind.

It's sad what happens to men when greed comes a knock-ing. It's always the women who pay.

"Maybe I can return the dress?" I ask Grace, waiting for Amaryllis. "It's too fancy for me. Not really my style."

"That's what I tried to tell him." Grace moves over to her sewing chair and a basket filled with notions. Inside, she gathers a few things. "I'd be careful if I were you. Men like Mr. Weston are only looking out for themselves."

There is more truth in her words than she realizes. "You get it dirty?" Grace reaches into her sewing basket.

"No ma'am," I say.

With a huff, Grace holds out her hand. "You can leave it, but I don't do exchanges. Especially when it hasn't been paid for."

I set the dress box down on a rocking chair by the window.

"What is this for?" I take the notions, careful not to stick myself with the sewing needle.

"To fix that Grace Adler knock-off you were sporting at church the other day. Which I will point out didn't come from my shop, and therefore don't even ask me to alter it. But I will suggest you find some lace and another layer of fabric to make it respectable before you go wearing it again. Unless, of course, you were trying to show off your boots to half the eligible bachelors in town."

"Grace, I—"

She cuts me off before I can say another word. "I would offer you some lace and a fabric piece, but I'm out and waiting for the next shipment to come in. It'll be nice once the railroad comes through. We won't have to wait so long to get things from the east."

"I wouldn't count on it." It seems living up in the mountains has its disadvantages. Am I the only one who didn't know about the railroad? Well, they better not get their hopes up, because there is no way the railroad is getting its hands on my claim. They will have to find another way through or around the mountain because I am not budging. Tail Feathers and his tribe are too important to let an iron horse cause a war.

Amaryllis comes out from behind the screen and grins. "There will be a lot of men coming to town. The mayor will have to change the name to Woodville."

Grace makes a strange noise in the back of her throat. Amaryllis has no filter. She waves her hand as she talks. "Come, *Jolene*, we have a closet to raid."

I don't have to ask who spilled the beans and told her my Christian name. "You know what? I think I'll be fine on my own."

"Nonsense." Amaryllis hooks her arm around mine.

"You'd be better off showing your boots than in anything from that one." Grace points out as I stumble through the door. I tuck the thread with a sewing needle and thimble in my pocket as we go.

Amaryllis keeps her arm hooked around mine as if we're the best of friends. We head for the saloon as another bout of rain spills from the sky. April in Deadwood is turning out to be nothing but one big, soggy mess. I can only hope things are much stronger up in the mountains that they, too, don't start falling apart. I have got to get back there soon.

"We should have done this the first time. Once I'm done dressing you up for Mr. Fancy Pants. It will probably hurt his feelings for you not to wear the dress he bought you." And she doesn't sound at all disappointed in the knowledge. Oh no, in fact, I think she's quite excited to see his reaction.

10

There's hardly anyone in the saloon this early in the day. I hesitate at the swinging door. A shiver travels down my spine.

Glen, the saloon owner, stands behind the bar polishing glasses. He's a stout man with beady little eyes under a bowler hat. I don't know what feels more uncomfortable as his gaze lifts: the way he stares at me or the fact the last time I saw my father alive, I was inside this sinful establishment. Tilting my chin up, I swallow down my unease, or maybe it's my pride.

I keep ending up in all the wrong places for a girl like me. Lord help me if anyone should see me and get the wrong idea, but I've been in here and have a feeling I'll be back again. I've never been one to care what others think. Maybe it's the way Glen is looking at me that causes me to doubt my actions. I shouldn't be here. What *will* others think?

I shake my head and go along with Amaryllis. I'm not the one in the wrong here. Amaryllis tugs me closer to Glen. I put my heels in the floor, but it does me no good.

Glen pauses, puts down the glass I'm sure is more polished than dry, and sets his gaze on me. I lick my dry lips, more nervous than needing a drink. It's not the nervous I get around the gambler or even the bounty hunter. It's an eerie feeling, like all the moisture in the air has been sucked out.

"Recruiting a new girl?"

"About time!" comes a call down the bar. I jump, startled. I didn't see the old timer standing and sipping at a drink.

"Don't get your hopes up." Amaryllis says. "She's promised to Mr. Weston. He won her fair and square at the poker game from old Earl."

"He ain't married her yet," Glen grunts, a frown turning his pudgy lips downward. I keep my mouth shut, afraid whatever I'd say would offend them. The very thought of being manhandled in this place makes my skin crawl.

"Oh, he will." Amaryllis winks. "She's playing hard to get, but once I get her hooked up with the right dress, won't be a man in town not trying to tie her down inside the church." She looks at me, her smile widening. "Including none other than a certain bounty hunter." She wiggles her perfectly sculpted brows.

My face turns on fire, and she laughs.

Glen tilts up his chin, his eyes narrowing on me, and whatever he's thinking, I don't like it. More so, I don't like the way he's looking at me, as if he's imagining things I'd rather not assume.

"Oh shoot!" the old timer in the bar shouts. "You sure you can't wrangle this one into dancing with us a few nights this week?"

Amaryllis scoots down by the old timer. "You don't like my dancing moves anymore, Clem?" She leans in and I can't hear what she says in the old man's ear, but it makes him chuckle.

Glen picks up another glass. "Heard the sheriff won't let you leave town."

Keeping my lips sealed, I glance over at Amaryllis. I should turn and leave and forget her offer, then I think the wiser. Glen owns the bar. He was here that night when my father gambled away our land and my hand in marriage.

"Did you see anything the night my father was killed?" I'm purposely ignoring his earlier question.

He twists the towel inside the glass and regards me. "Men die when they can't ante up on their promises. Your father isn't the first to meet his end back in the alley. I reckon you'll have to settle his debts before you leave town."

I can only think of one debt my father had, and that was to Chief Tail Feathers and his tribe. Although I wouldn't put it past Earl to borrow a few dollars to get in on the poker game.

"And what debts would you be talking about?" I'm curious.

Glen puts down the glass and the cloth. He plants his elbows on the bar. He's a big guy, broad shoulders, and an equally broad chest with an even wider belly. There is a gap between his teeth the size of a small prairie, and it shows when he grins. "Why don't you come in the back with me and we can discuss it."

Did he just? No… I open my mouth. Close it. I'm about to say something not very lady-like when Amaryllis comes to my rescue. "Sorry, Glen, she's mine. You'll have to wait. Give Clem a round on me."

With that, she yanks me to the stairs, covered in an old tattered oriental print rug that's nailed to the wooden steps. Supposedly, it adds a little class to the place. All the while, I can feel the stare on my back, but I refuse to acknowledge it.

Does Glen know about the railroad? Is that why he made a pass at me? Or is it something else? Does my father have other debts I don't know about? Is one of them to Glen? And if so, what is it I'm going to have to do to pay him?

As we top the stairs, I follow Amaryllis to her room. It's at the end of the hall, the last room to the right. She beckons me inside, but I stand there, letting Glen's words sink in my mind.

Am I even obligated to pay my father's debts? The man is dead.

But in my heart, I hear a brief whisper saying it's the right thing to do.

At this rate, I'll be stuck in town and in my father's debt for the rest of my life.

Inside her room, Amaryllis stands in front of a large armoire pulling out dresses left and right. There's a dressing screen with black wood and red velvet material in the corner. It wasn't there when I was here before. The room seems smaller with the bed in the middle and the washstand by the window. Behind the dressing panel is a cot where Robbie sleeps. It's been moved from the end of the bed. Heaven above, I hope Amaryllis isn't entertaining while the boy is in the corner sleeping.

I shake my head at the thoughts as she whirls around and holds up a deep green gown. She comes marching toward me and I try to back up.

"It'll go with your eyes," she tries, pressing the gown against me.

I stretch my neck, feeling weird as she hums and haws, then clucks her tongue. "You're busty, and while I am sure the gambler will thank me for the view, I can't have you falling entirely out." She tosses the dress on the bed behind me. "I might wear that one tonight."

She sorts through more dresses. There must be at least a dozen hanging in the large armoire. It's plain, which surprises me. With the oriental carpet and the dressing screen, I would have thought the furniture more distinguished.

"I appreciate you offering to share your dresses, but it's really unnecessary."

She waves her hand and glances through the dresses again. "You're doing me a favor, really. I've been meaning to hand off a few older ones. Did you see the one Grace is fitting for me?"

She's bent and I try not to look straight at her, or should I say her, behind. I glance around at the faded paper on the wall and its large green leaves with yellow roses. They're painted, and they're as lovely as the dress at Grace's. I tell her so.

"Well, I can't keep wearing the same ones over and over. You know the customers like to see something new now and again."

She turns back to me, this time with a blue frock. It's out of style, simple, but not any more modest than the first.

"I thought I had this in here somewhere. When I saw the navy the gambler chose for you, I knew blue was your color." She beamed. "Here, try it on."

"I couldn't." Not here. I wince, looking around.

"Go on, behind the screen."

"I don't know."

She gives me a look, and I know I'm not getting out of there without trying on this dress.

She presses towards me again. "At least with this one you won't have to worry about showing too much of those cowboy boots. Unless you want to." She says, "I hitch mine up a little when I'm dancing. Not just the ankles, mind you, but men, they like a little leg now and again."

I step back, feeling it's getting a little too warm in here, and I don't like where the conversation is going. I stumble, step on something, and land on the bed. Amaryllis kicks the obstacle to the side with a huff.

It's a boot.

No. It's not just any boot. It's my father's boot!

I right myself on the bed, the dress forgotten. It falls as I stand and move to pick up the boot. Amaryllis catches the dress before it hits the floor.

"Why is this here?" I ask.

"You'd be amazed, Toots, at the things I find in my room

the morning after." She waves it away. "Now try on this dress. I think you'll be surprised."

Surprised is right.

"What was my father doing in your room?" I check out the boot, risk putting my hand inside, and find it's empty. Of course, it would be. Why would it have anything else inside it?

Amaryllis pales a little under her face paint. She shakes out the dress from any wrinkles it might have gotten on its travels south to the floor. "I suppose we are both adults, so there is no harm in telling you that your father came to my room many times on his visits into town."

"I see," I say slowly. My hands wrap around the boot. "But how did his boot get here? He was wearing it when they found him dead in the alley."

Amaryllis's grip tightens on the dress. "Are you sure?"

I nod.

"The old fool had one boot in his hand and the other on his foot when he went stumbling out of here that morning. I honestly don't even know how you recognize it as his."

"I take care of my father. I have all my life. I'd know his boots anywhere." I twist the old worn leather in my hand. It gives no resistance, and I feel another piece of me crack inside for the man who raised me. Mean as he was, I still loved him.

"I know all about your momma leaving." Amaryllis sits on the bed. Still holding the blue dress, she pats on the coverlet beside her.

Hesitant at first, I gradually lower back down on the bed. I try not to think of all the overnight guests she may have entertained on this very mattress where I sit. I grip the boot, curious and angry at the same time.

"Your father has been coming up here for years, Toots. He gets drunk, he talks, he cries for *her*." I detect a bitterness in her voice. "Always for her."

By *her*, I believe she refers to my mother.

"He promised me. Used to tell me all the time he would pack me up and take me up to that mountain and make an honest woman of me. I knew he never would. He's still married to her, you know. Fool man." She reaches up to wipe the moisture building against her lashes and catches it before it messes up her powered cheeks.

There is so much I want to ask, to say, and I don't know where to start. Amaryllis cares about my father. She sniffles and puts her hand over mine. "I would have never tried to replace her. Robbie. He needs a good man to lead by example."

I hold back the snort building up. Earl is... was anything but a good example.

"Robbie. Is he?" Somehow, I can't finish asking, but Amaryllis senses what I want to know.

She shakes her head. "I had Robbie before I came to work for Glen. Back then, it was Jasmine who oversaw the girls here. Her family came across the sea, and men lined up outside to dance with her. She took me under her wing and gave me a roof and a place for Robbie when I had none. She placed my hand in Earl's and told me to dance. He was the first man I ever danced with."

Her eyes glaze, and she's far away, living in a memory. I stare straight ahead at the dresses heaped on the floor, at the washstand with powder and lip paint and eye color smeared near the porcelain basin.

I don't want to think of my father with anyone else. I run my thumb over the worn toe of the boot. "Did you know he kept a photo of her in his boot? Gave him satisfaction now and then to know he was stepping on her face."

Amaryllis laughed. "Sounds like Earl."

"Yeah."

And she left it at that.

A knock comes to the door and a woman not much older than me peeks her head in. She has blood-red curls, the color of an evening sunset. "You've got a caller downstairs. Glen says to get your arse down to the bar. Oh, and you owe Clem a private dance."

Then she notices me, standing taller. "Glen said nothing about taking on a new girl."

"I'm not." I get to my feet, holding Earl's old worn boot.

"She's a friend. Tell Glen to keep his pants on, I'll be down shortly."

The redhead nods and closes the door.

"Take the dress. It will be a lot less work than that pink catastrophe you wore on Sunday."

Is there anyone who hasn't heard about seeing my cowboy boots?

11

It's almost lunch when I come across Ella Mae hanging off Lincoln's arm. Her cheeks are flushed, and several strands of her hair are out of place. Normally, Ella Mae keeps her hair all pulled and pinned back.

Lincoln bends near her, says something in her ear that turns her flush to a full-on red cheeked blush. She titters and turns to him when he freezes. They're standing on the other side of his horse in the street. His eyes lift and his gaze finds me. Clearing his throat, he says, "Mrs. Weston."

"It's Jo Dean, thank you very much."

Ella gasps as she acknowledges me. "Jo. Where have you been?"

I show her the dress.

Lincoln slides Ella Mae's hand from his arm. "I have to be returning to the ranch. It was good to see you again, and you." He pauses, swallows hard, and says, "Jo."

I can't imagine it took all his might to break manners and call me something other than "Miss Dean."

Ella Mae pouts as she watches him step away and mount

his horse. He waves as he rides down the street and Ella stands watching him for several moments.

I lean into her. "Someone's out on a stroll without a chaperone."

She scowls at me, and I laugh. "I'm surprised Mr. Weston hasn't carried you kicking and screaming in front of my father yet."

"I'm sure he'll try."

Ella Mae sighs, looks at me and then the dress. "You know Momma said she'd help fix the other one. I suppose you'll be wearing them a lot more often, with Mr. Weston claiming you for a wife. What happened to the fancy dress he bought you? I didn't take you for the daring type." Her eyes go to the bodice flung over my arm.

I tell her about my visit to Grace's, which led me to Amaryllis as we walk back to the boarding house. Ruby has got hot water and tea in the kitchen. We sit in the parlor while no one else is around to disturb us.

"You've got to be careful." Ella Mae adds a little more honey to her tea.

"I could say the same thing about you. Does your father know you were out alone with Lincoln?"

Ella Mae rolls her eyes. "I was on my way to meet you, and we weren't alone." She reaches and tucks a hair behind her ear. She's wearing another gingham dress, with her tea saucer on her lap and her hands around her cup. "Besides, don't you worry about me and Lincoln. We're going to be married one day."

"He asked you?"

"He will. He says he loves me."

Even I know a man can say he loves you and not offer you a ring. Chitto comes to mind, and I'm tempted to ask my best friend if her rancher has brought her a set of ponies and tied them to the porch. Chitto showing up in town has made me more nervous. On top of that, I'm supposed to meet the bounty hunter at the mercantile this afternoon, and I've been trying to avoid the gambler. He's persistent. While I was out, he left a note on my door with another invitation to dinner. I don't know what makes my stomach knot more: that he was at my door or having dinner with him.

"I don't want to see you get hurt." And I mean what I say.

"I'm more worried about you. Word has it you're postponing the wedding to find your father's killer, but in the meantime, you're traipsing in the bathhouse and visiting the saloon."

I sit back on the wingback chair and grin. "Don't you worry about me. I've got Shorty."

"Please tell me that isn't the name of one of your horses," Ella Mae says.

I snort. "Shorty's Pa's gun."

"The only gun I knew your father had was that old sawed-off shotgun he threatened my father with last summer."

I remember. The good reverend tried to get Earl sober and talk him into giving up drinking firewater. Earl pulled out Shorty and waved it for Reverend Carter to get out of the way.

"That's the one."

"You can't have it on you," Ella Mae whispers, glancing toward the doorway as the sound of a door opens and closes.

One of the other boarders walks past, paying us no mind.

"It's tucked under my mattress." I glance upstairs. "You don't think I'm not going to protect myself with a killer on the loose, do you?"

Ella Mae sits her tea on the little table between our chairs. "Has the sheriff found any fresh evidence to support your case against the gambler?"

I shake my head.

Ella Mae takes my hand. "Jo, I know you want to find your father's killer, and the sheriff won't let you go home yet, but do you really want to return to those mountains?"

I bite my lip. Ella Mae is my best friend, and I hate keeping secrets from her.

"I heard the railroad is buying up land in the mountain and Lincoln said there is only one spot for them to dig and come through the gulch. He says your claim is a gold mine."

Gold mine in more than one way. I tell her all about the meeting with the railroad gentlemen at the hotel.

"Have you thought of anyone else who would want Earl dead? You said yourself Amaryllis had your father's boot in her room. What if she tried to kill him for the claim paper to the land?"

I tap a finger against Ruby's fine china teacup. "I don't think so. She was sincerely hurt over his death. I even left the boot. My father kept things in his boots, and if he had anything in there, it's gone."

"Maybe she took it."

"I don't think so," I say. "The gambler has an IOU from my father for his half of our mine. He needs to marry me to get full access, but I'm already one step ahead of him."

"Oh, Jo. What have you done now?" Ella Mae knows me too well.

I open my mouth to tell her and realize in doing so I would have to tell her about Chitto and his tribe living near our claim on Standing Rock.

I take a large gulp of tea and swallow the hot liquid. I blink while the liquid scorches my throat.

"Oh, no, you don't." Ella Mae pulls the teacup from my hand. "Does this have to do with the bounty hunter?"

I press my lips tight together.

"What if the bounty hunter is the one who killed your father?"

Ella Mae's words take me by surprise. I hadn't thought of him. For a moment, I consider it. Then the facts rule it out.

"He wasn't in town that night. He came in that morning with a bounty on his horse."

"Wasn't your father shot in the morning?" She gives me that look, challenging my thoughts.

"Yes, but my father didn't have a bounty on his head."

"True. You've got Amaryllis and the bounty hunter. Who else was there or could have done it?"

"The gambler." I practically growl his name. He's got gold in his eyes, flecks of dollars, and I'm his ticket to wealth. It should burn my gut. So why does the image of the man's emerald greens turn my insides to mush?

I am not about to let him weaken me with fancy dinners, drinks, and gazes filled with a kind of longing Ella Mae's father warns us all about in church.

"Mr. Weston. You can call him that, you know?"

Then I tilt my head and see where this is going. "He's got you hogtied and blinded with his wily words."

Ella Mae sighs deeply. "He may have said something to Lincoln and me this morning when we were strolling through town. He stepped out of the hotel with Miss Davenport and her father. I think they were headed to the claims office."

Another place on my list. I touch the side of my temple. It throbs when I think of all the places and people I need to see and what other debts to settle.

"Glen at the saloon."

"What about him?"

"He says my father has debts. When I asked him about them, he invited me in the back to discuss them."

"There is nothing good coming from a man taking a proper young woman as yourself in the back of that kind of establishment." Ruby waltzes into the parlor. She holds two slices of cake in our direction.

"Oh, thank you," Ella Mae exclaims. She has a soft spot for a good, thick slice of cake.

"You still trying to find your father's killer?" Ruby sits the plates on the little table between us. "Anything new?"

"That's what I asked," Ella Mae says.

"Nothing that the sheriff will consider evidence," I chime in.

"Well, you ladies enjoy your cake. Chord told me this morning he's going to be sticking around a few more days and I have a feeling he might be after the same killer. Although, I can't imagine why as there is no bounty on finding your father's killer." Ruby winks and hums as she leaves us.

Ella Mae stuffs her face with cake as politely as any preacher's daughter can. I join her, my mind rolls around names in my head.

"You going to eat your cake or keep thinking too hard?"

I eat my cake.

Ella Mae is right. The gambler might be guilty of swindling and cheating, but he already has my father's IOU. According to the sheriff, Buck had someone vouch for him. Maybe one of the Swanson sisters or a dancing girl at the saloon. With my luck it could have been Lincoln who did it. Either way, that leaves Amaryllis, who I have ruled out on my own.

I suppose I need to talk to Jed Warner at the hotel. That is, if I can get him away from Daphne Davenport. Perhaps having dinner with the gambler this evening will bring me one step closer to sealing a deal of my own.

12

Later in the afternoon, Ella Mae walks along with me to the mercantile. She chats away about lace and dresses, and I know she's dreaming of a wedding with Lincoln. We cross the street to avoid the hotel and the saloon. The sky above it is a dreary blue with clouds drifting away from the sun. I tilt my hat down, glad I wore it, and keep my eyes on my boots.

"You should wear a bonnet when you put on a dress again," Ella Mae says.

"No, thank you." I like my wide-brimmed hat. Earl brought it home one day, saying he found it cast off by a stream. It didn't suit him, but it fit me just fine.

"It's a good thing you're promised to get married, else I can't imagine trying to attract a man. Now, Lincoln, he likes a woman who knows how to cook." And she goes on and on about Lincoln. The poor girl has it bad.

The closer we get to the saloon and hotel, a piece of me eases. At least there is no sight of the gambler. I wonder for a moment where he is and what he is doing, but then stop myself. It's none of my business. Why should I care?

Lord above, please tell me I haven't become like Ella Mae and got all cow-eyed for the man. I take a deep breath, think of him, and sure enough, there's a spark of something there. It's small, and maybe it'll grow, maybe it won't. I'm allowed to care; I just don't want to fall for his tricks. It burns my brisket knowing he's after the big payout for our claim.

Maybe they killed the wrong Dean. Then it strikes me, and I stop. Ella Mae walks on a few feet before she realizes I'm not there. She turns back and says, "What's the matter?"

"What if this was all a plan?"

"Plan? To go to the Jensen's for supplies?"

I glance back at the saloon. "They had to kill him." I step up and lower my voice, "Don't you see? Kill Earl, and marry me, and you get control of the entire deed for our claim."

Okay, maybe the thought crossed my mind already. Speaking it out loud causes a chill in my bones.

Who would do that?

"Then you can rule out the gambler for sure," Ella Mae says.

"You like him, you marry him."

She laughs and shakes her head. "I have got Lincoln. Maybe we can have a double wedding. Oh, Jo, wouldn't that be so nice?"

"No."

And she frowns. I didn't mean to hurt her feelings. "The gambler won't stay in town for long," I explain. "He'll cash out and move on, that's what they do."

"Then on second thought," Ella Mae picks up her skirts to avoid a scraggly mutt laying in front of the bank. "We'd best find you a way out of having to marry him. I don't want you to go."

The only place I plan on going is back up to the mountains. I hope Chitto took my advice and left town before anyone discovered him.

We don't get to speculate any further, for Ella Mae bumps

against me. She nods ahead and I bite my lip. My stomach twists, this time in a good way.

Leaning against the side of the mercantile with a boot against the wall and his arms crossed is the bounty hunter.

"Ladies." The bounty hunter tips his hat and gives me a long stare with those penetrating slate-colored eyes.

"Good afternoon." Ella Mae grins. "Have you decided to stay a bit, Mr. Townes? Father mentioned wanting to ask you over for supper."

Is she crazy? Does she know the bounty hunter tracks men for money?

She bats those lashes, and I know she's up to something.

I step away from them and head into the mercantile. "Sorry, but I've got business to attend."

Ella Mae waves her hand. "You'll have to excuse my best friend. She was raised in the mountains alone with her father."

My ears burn as I bite down the words forming on my tongue.

Inside the mercantile, Jensen is busy packing a young woman's basket with canned goods and sacks of sugar and flour. Around her skirt is a chubby-cheeked little darling blinking up at me with the prettiest blue eyes.

The woman is younger than me. A mail-order bride, perhaps? Those who ride into Dakota Territory looking for gold stay but a few winters and head for the mountains or further west.

Her faded red hair matches the rosiness of her nose and cheeks. Apparently, no one told the woman to keep her bonnet on.

"There you are, Mrs. Duncan. You need any help to get back to your wagon?" Jensen asks.

"No, I'll be fine, thank you," she stammers, glancing as the door opens and the bounty hunter's wide frame fills the doorway. He's a sight, my bounty hunter.

Thinking of him that way warms my insides. I glance away, afraid soon my face will show it's getting too hot inside my clothes. It's spring and the weather's warm. Soon, it'll get hot, and I'll be back up in my stream wading and catching fish.

With Earl gone, Chitto won't let me live alone. Seeing Mrs. Duncan and her little one head toward the bounty hunter sends a yearning inside me I never thought I'd have. Children. What kind of mother would I make not having one of my own?

As if he could read my thoughts from my face, the bounty hunter raises an eyebrow. He steps out of the way and scoops up the basket before Mrs. Duncan can protest.

"You don't have to," she teeters on the edge of a giggle.

"Always happy to help a pretty lady." He reaches down with his other arm and scoops up that pretty blue-eyed baby.

He's never called me pretty. I fume, grinding my bootheel in the floor as he leaves with Mrs. Duncan at his side and a baby in his arms. For a man who hunts outlaws, the picture of him being a family man suits him. Maybe too much.

Behind the counter, Jensen clears his throat.

My nostrils flare as Ella Mae comes around the aisle with lace in her hands.

"What can I do for you?" Jensen asks.

"I've come to pick up my order you've been so kindly holding for me."

Jensen goes pale. He wipes his hands down the apron around his waist. "You leaving town?"

"I don't believe that's anyone's business but mine. I'll have the horses hitched and the wagon ready to go in an hour. That should be enough time for you to get my supplies ready for loading."

"I didn't think you'd be coming this soon to get it. I'm afraid you'll have to wait until the supply wagon comes back into town."

"What do you mean? I paid for those supplies. You had them here when I bought them."

He holds up his hands. "I did, but I sold them to the railroad for the men camped on the other side of the mountain pass."

"You sold my supplies!" My heart thuds like a team of wild horses. No! My eyes flick around, trying to find something to latch on.

I'm about to reach over and grab Jensen by the shirt collars, when a hand firmly but gently goes around my waist and pulls me back. "What matter of trouble are you causing, Dimples?"

"Dimples?" I croak. How could he call me that? I told him not to do that! Didn't I? And in front of everyone in the entire store? Okay, Jensen and Ella Mae.

I whip around, his arm keeping his hold on my waist. Lord have mercy on me, I pray. If the town wasn't gossiping before, it will now. Jensen and his wife are good ones to get it started.

"What's the problem?" The bounty hunter ignores me and asks Jensen.

"She wants supplies I don't got."

"I paid for them." I ball my hands into fists.

Ella Mae gasps but stays out of it.

"Is this right?" the bounty hunter asks.

"It is. She couldn't pick them up when I had them ready. Said she'd come back for them when she could leave town. I sold them to the railroad. She'll have to wait until the next supply wagon comes."

"And when is that?" The bounty hunter flexes his fingers against my pant-clad hips. It's distracting, and I try to swat his hand away. His grip tightens. A warning.

I bite my lip and glare at Jensen.

"Next supply wagon comes next month, but I imagine the railroad will wipe me clean again as long as they're working on getting the track laid. Once the railroad comes through, though," Jensen scratches his balding head. "Deliveries will come more frequent and new stuff from the east."

"I don't care about the east." I grit my teeth between each word.

"Is there anything here of the order you can fill?" The bounty hunter remains calm, poised, and I'm wound like a cougar about to spring.

Jensen rubs a hand down the side of his face, looks behind him, and around, then snaps his fingers. "I got some flour and sugar and canned beans. I wouldn't let the railroad take it all, you know. Folks around here need to eat."

"Tobacco. I need the tobacco." I strain to hold in the words and say them politely.

Jensen shrugs. "Figured your pa died, you wouldn't need it anymore. I sold the last to Glen over at the saloon. Imagine you could see if he'd sell it to you. Never known a woman to need tobacco."

I don't, but I can't tell him that. Jensen gives me the once-over, takes in my pants, my boots, and of course comes back up to my hat.

He mutters something under his breath, and the bounty hunter moves me to the side.

"She gave you money for supplies."

Jensen pulls out his ledger and gets even more pale. "Well, yes. I recorded the credit for her right here."

"Pay the lady." The bounty hunter reaches into his long coat and pushes it back to allow the butt of his gun to show.

"I'm afraid there isn't any credit left," Jensen's voice goes hoarse.

"What do you mean 'there isn't any credit left?" My fist pounds down on the table. "What happened to my money?"

"Your husband's been coming in the past few days charging

against the account." He points to the numbers going down the column.

"I don't have a husband."

Ella Mae steps up beside me. "Jo isn't married."

Jensen goes almost white. "But you married Mr. Weston. He came in buying cigars and traveling supplies."

"I knew it," I seethe out loud. "That worthless, swindling, no good…"

"You already said that," Ella Mae points out.

"Calm, Dimples." The bounty hunter gives me a stern look.

"He's guilty." And here I'd been giving him the benefit of doubt. "Why else would he be leaving town?"

"We'll deal with the leaving town later," the bounty hunter says. "But right now, there is a matter of Miss Dean's account. Whatever purchases Mr. Weston has made, you'll need to record a new column in your accounts book and remove those charges from Miss Dean to Mr. Weston."

"I don't give credit to strangers." Jensen bristles.

He didn't mind giving someone else my money, I want to say, but I don't. I bite my lip and try to find my calm.

"Clearly there's been a misunderstanding," Ella Mae chimes in.

"Yes, like taking the word of a stranger over someone who's been coming here for years." Pretty much my entire life.

The bounty hunter raises his hand for me to quiet. I scowl at him, crossing my arms, as my gaze lands on the butt of that six shooter he's got strapped to his thigh.

My oh my, the man has thick thighs. I would do well not to look at them. I divert my gaze to Ella Mae. She smiles faintly.

"Everyone in town has been talking about you wed'n Mr. Weston," Jensen huffs.

"Shame on you, Mr. Jensen, listening and believing gossip," Ella Mae says.

"Fix the accounts." The bounty hunter is running thin on patience. I can see it in the way his jaw has gotten tense.

Mr. Jensen twists his lips and scrunches up his face, making his brows come together in an ugly manner. Finally, he takes his pencil and tallies the charges. He places them in a new column under the gambler's name and scratches out the debt from mine.

"Now, about those supplies?" the bounty hunter asks.

Without them, I can't pay my debt to Tail Feathers. Chitto will come back and the other few families waiting on supplies will come raiding our claim in retaliation.

"I can't give you what I don't have."

I look to the ceiling. Why, oh why, Lord, is this happening to me?

I got nothing. No money, no supplies, no father, and soon no choice other than marrying the gambler.

I let them all down. Chitto. Tail Feathers. Earl. Even the woman who abandoned me as a child. It's raining pity, and this time I'm the one about to get buried if I can't find my father's killer soon.

I follow Ella Mae out on the porch. It's getting past the time her mother will want her home to help with preparing for supper, and she's skipped out on her chores most of the day to spend it with me.

It comes as no surprise when Reverend Carter crosses the street and tells her they're going home.

At least I should be thankful Earl never treated me that way, a woman should be able to do what she wants when she wants. Especially since she's marrying age. Maybe someday.

The bounty hunter steps back outside. I look over at him and my hat slides down the back of my hair. "What do we do now?" I ask.

"I'll talk to Glen, see if he can throw in a few bottles of whiskey to smooth things over."

I crinkle my nose at hearing the word whiskey. I have no doubt Tail Feathers will be happy to accept some firewater in compensation for his wait. "But I don't have any money."

"How are you staying at the boarding house?"

I roll back my shoulders. "I do kitchen work and clean rooms."

The bounty hunter nods. "I wondered why you had such a small room tucked away from the rest. No matter. Glen can settle with Jensen. I'll make sure of it."

He sounds like he would, and it did this funny thing inside me. I like the way this man talks. He takes charge, and it tickles my bones. I can't help wondering what it would be like to have him give me a few sweet commands. My eyes land on his lips, and they grimace.

He walks around me. "Stay out of trouble tonight, will you?"

"I'm having dinner at the hotel."

That stops him in his tracks. He glances back. "With Weston?"

"Of course." I smooth my hands down over my pant-clad hips to wipe the guilt sweat away.

The bounty hunter narrows his gaze. They're not intense like the gambler. They don't sparkle and flirt. Oh, no. The bounty hunter is all business. The way he's looking at me, I'd say I'm in his scope of business. It does a funny thing to a girl. It heats my insides and I lick my lips. I'm as bad as Ella Mae is over Lincoln. No. Not quite. Ella Mae's in love, and I... well, I'm just admiring the view.

Besides, I'm bound to marry another, thanks to a piece of paper and the law of the land. I have to get rid of one suitor before I can think of another.

And, thinking of suitors, I need to get back to the boarding house and fix me up a dress before dinner at the hotel.

The bounty hunter gives me an odd look. Down the way

comes several ladies carrying baskets and heading to the mercantile. A wagon goes down the street, and for a moment there, the world has stopped.

Then the bounty hunter breaks the silence. "If he tries to get you to go upstairs, don't. Or better yet, have dinner with Ruby tonight at the boarding house."

I have no intention of going anywhere private with the gambler. I know how sly the man can be. He swindled my father, and he's been up to no good trying to swindle others around town. Or maybe just me.

"I would, but the gambler left me a note and invited me. Besides, I want to talk to Jed Warner. He might know something about my father's killer."

"The sheriff has already talked to him."

"But he might not have told him everything. I'll hear it for myself. You worry about getting that tobacco up the mountain, as is our deal."

His lips twitch and, for a second, I see a glimmer in those slate-colored eyes. "Yes, ma'am." He tilts his hat and is on his way.

Down at the telegraph office, I spot Mr. Davenport and the gambler. Hurriedly, I make my way back to the other side of the walk and to the boarding house. I've got to prepare myself before I can confront the gambler.

Mrs. Weston. I would laugh, but my stomach sours, and a mixed feeling of regret and longing strike me at once. Odd. I can't explain it more than that, but it has me practically running for Ruby's place.

13

"Pierce Weston," I say, standing in front of the mirror. I pull my hair up, trying to decide what to do with it. "Mrs. Pierce Weston. Jo Weston."

There's a lift of a smile there as I give in and dream for a moment about what it would be like to marry the gambler. My heart skips as I envision those emerald-green eyes staring back at me. Men like the gambler are looking for wives more like Miss Davenport. I let my hair fall down my back, feeling less exposed this way. The dress Amaryllis gave me is daring and beautiful all the same. It dips as low in the back as it does in the front. My poor sisters squish together in the front, lifting them to attention. Thank goodness Grace gave me sewing supplies. Ruby dug in her stash and came up with a bit of lace to keep the sisters from being exposed.

It took almost all the rest of the afternoon to help her in the kitchen and find the lace.

I sigh, turning to the side. I'm no grand beauty. Not like my mother. I glance at her picture. All I can feel for the woman is the sourness thoughts of her leaves in my mouth.

Would she even care to know Earl was gone?

Obviously, she never cared about me. I take the photo and turn it away, so I no longer see her face. Earl always said I reminded him of her. I don't see it. Her nose is too slim and her lips too full. I can't remember the color of her eyes, but Earl always said they were the color of a viper.

With that, I grab a piece of ribbon, another find in Ruby's stash. I tie up my hair and pull the shawl around to cover myself.

There's a tap at my door. My stomach about bottoms out as I hear, "Your gentleman caller is here."

"Be right down."

I look back in the mirror, but it's not those emerald eyes I'm envisioning staring back at me. They're stone cold grey, and they make me shiver. Why is it I have such a reaction to both of these men?

Maybe I'm more like my mother than I want to admit. But not tonight.

I'm on a mission and I can't let either man distract me. Guilt creeps up as I leave my room and pass the one where I know the bounty hunter sleeps. I pull back my shoulders, careful not to trip on my skirt on the stairs, and find Pierce Weston, the gambler, waiting for me.

It looks like he's got a shave recently.

"I had expected to see you in the traveling dress."

"Is that a problem?" I ask, very much aware of the way he's looking at me. He tugs on his suit lapels, and he's in the same pin striped one from the first night when my father was alive.

"No." He steps closer to me in the foyer. Behind him, the light of the late evening sun sends shadows across the wood floor. "When I thought you couldn't look any prettier than the day before. What's this?" He touches the ribbon holding my hair up. "You might not be my wife, yet, Jolene, but you are far from a schoolgirl."

My breath catches in my throat as he pulls the ribbon and releases my hair. As the gambler gets closer, I can smell the rich scents of aftershave, but beneath, there's something softer, more feminine. Jasmine. Where else have I caught that scent? Perhaps the bathhouse, I think as my hair cascades down my back. The gambler tucks the ribbon in his pocket and holds his arm for me to take.

"Beautiful. Shall we go?"

"You've been to the bathhouse today?" I say it to pull myself out of the fantasy that the gambler is anything but a killer and crook.

"One's appearance and hygiene are of utmost importance. I believe you recently visited for a bath?" His brows go up and he's got me there. The idea of one of the Swanson sisters assisting him with a bath burns in my gut as much as it bothers me to think of Emma Swanson seeing parts of the bounty hunter I haven't.

Gah!! It isn't any of my business. Except now the bounty hunter and I have a deal, so I feel like it does. And the gambler is technically my future husband. I press my lips together, not liking the situation I've gotten myself into. There is only one way to choose between these men.

And that's proving one of them is a killer. Or at the very least, a no-good cheating swindler. I told the bounty hunter I'd stay out of trouble.

Lord help me, I just might have lied. Because trouble in Deadwood is impossible to avoid.

"I'm looking forward to dinner. I believe we have a lot to discuss," I say, as he opens the door and leads me outside.

The sun is lowering, and the air is warmer than what I'm used to living in the mountains for spring.

I see several shop owners turning their signs to lock up. Horses stand tied in front of the saloon, and people are heading to supper, whether at home or at the cafe or hotel.

"I was hoping you'd let me apologize. I do not want our time together to be spent bickering like an old married couple. Especially, since you have been putting me off from completing the ceremony."

The gambler tips his hat to a passing couple. When we come to the hotel, Sherman is at the desk. He averts his gaze when he looks up and spots us. There are candles and white tablecloths on each of the tables in the dining room. The smell of beeswax invades my senses first.

"The staff has been cleaning all day." The gambler wrinkles his nose. "Mr. Warner wants the place spotless before the spring festival. Is that something you think you'd enjoy? I've never been here for it."

I allow him to press his hand to my back and steer me through the tables. The waiter is walking our way, when I notice Mr. Davenport stand and beckon us to a large table in the far corner.

"Neither have I," I admit. "We usually come for supplies and leave. Earl isn't one for staying in town long."

"I see." The gambler pulls out a chair for me as we get to the table. It's already set for two. Across from us, Mr. Davenport, Daphne, and Mr. Conway dine. I take a quick glance around, hoping to spot Jed Warner and frown.

"Looking for someone? The bounty hunter perhaps?"

I shake my head, take a seat.

"I thought it would be best for the two of us to dine together. Alone." He takes a seat across from me. It doesn't pass my attention that across from me, the gambler has a good view of the Davenports and anyone entering the dining room.

We're close to the fireplace. A small crackling fire sends enough heat, so I allow my shawl to slide down from my shoulders. It's black lace and probably out of season, but who cares? Not I.

"I hear the pot roast is on special tonight," the gambler

says as a waiter comes near. "Is that what you'd like me to order?"

The waiter is a young man with his hair parted to the side and big curious brown eyes. He never gets to say a word, for the gambler orders a fancy drink while I interrupt and request water.

I don't wait for the man to leave before I ask, "Will this be going on my tab or yours?"

His jaw slacks for a second, then his mask is back on. Those emerald eyes flash at me, and I place my elbows on the table and lean forward.

"I don't know what you may have heard, darling, but have no fear. Order whatever you like. It's on me." The gambler looks at the waiter. "Pot roast."

I tilt my head, think for a moment, then say, "Steak. Medium Rare."

"Good choice," the waiter takes off and I keep my elbows on the table. The gambler has a twitch in his left eye.

"How was your day?" he asks.

"Funny you should ask," I answer.

He leans back with a serious expression on his face. "You were with the bounty hunter today, Mr. Townes. Tell me, darlin', do you think he is going to help find your father's killer? I understand you want justice serviced. It's the reason you've been avoiding us getting married. But I must say, it doesn't look good for a woman's reputation to spend so much time with another man when she's practically married."

I rest my chin on my hands. "Practically married? Or married? Seems a lot of folks in Deadwood think we're hitched already."

"As it should be." The gambler reaches for my hands, and I jerk them back away from him. As I do, the waiter brings our drinks. His arm crosses over the gamblers and with mine pulling out of the mix, the glass of water splashes against the sisters, running down my bodice, and landing in my lap.

I gasp. The gambler gets to his feet. The waiter fumbles to put down the other drink as the gambler grabs it. "Let's not go adding spilling wine, shall we? Especially one of this year."

My jaw slackens. I feel hands against my sisters and startle as the waiter presses a cloth napkin against my chest.

"I've got it!" I tell him. He's pressing and twisting, and I can feel the lace piece coming loose.

"I'm so sorry!" the waiter says. "Please let me help you."

"No. Really." I try to take hold of the napkin, to push him away. Another hand reaches in, and the waiter pulls back. While I hold the napkin, the waiter yanks back the lace, and the gambler's eyes widen. He turns to shield me from the waiter. In a blink of an eye, he has the lace in his hand, stuffing it in his pocket. "Go on with you, get the lady another drink. This time you'd best make it sherry."

"Oh dear." Daphne Davenport stands beside me. Her hand over her mouth. "How terrible. Are you alright?"

I grab my shawl and quickly wrap it around me. I stand and the gambler has an apologetic expression on his face.

"At least it's water," I say.

"There's a water closet further back. I'd offer to take you to my room, but I'm afraid you're a much larger size than I am." She titters and flutters her lashes at the gambler.

I spy Jed Warner coming from the back. He must have heard the commotion of the incident and came to check on his guest.

"I suppose I should go try to freshen up a bit. Excuse me." I head for the water closet when I notice the gambler coming behind me. "Oh no. You stay here. I'll be but a moment."

He glances at the Davenports, now watching us, as is every eye in the room. My neck is growing hot and if it weren't for the waiter giving me an opportunity to talk with Jed, I might be embarrassed.

Halfway there, I realize the gambler still has my piece of lace. When I go to turn back, I see him speaking with Conway and Davenport. Daphne seems to hang on his every word.

"Are you okay, Miss Dean?"

I turn at the sound of Jed Warner's voice. "I am. I was just heading to the water closet. Can you show me the way?"

"Of course." He points, and we head away from curious eyes. "I do apologize for my staff's clumsiness. Tonight, dinner is on me."

"That's kind of you, Mr. Warner." I'm not about to turn down a free meal any more than I am to let someone take the blame where it isn't entirely theirs. "I do appreciate it. I believe it was an accident on both or parts. Too many moving hands."

"All the same, I'd feel better covering your meal." Mr. Warner stops outside of a door. He's not wearing a jacket and his sleeves are rolled up to his elbows. He smells like pot roast and grease. I don't ask him who is doing the cooking. The man has enough things to deal with running a hotel, and I need him to focus during the few moments I have with him.

'I'd best be leaving you to—it." He seems to have his eyes glued on Daphne. It's the look of a starving wolf. Poor Daphne is his prey. I shiver and pull my shawl tighter despite the warmth in the room.

"May I ask you something?" My question brings his attention back to me.

"Yes?"

"The night my father died. You were playing in the card game."

Warner's jaw twitches a little. "We all gambled that night. Some of us took deeper losses than others."

"Do you really think the gam—Mr. Weston cheated?"

A perplexed expression crosses his face. There are circles

under his eyes, and he shoves his hands in his pockets. "Should you be asking me this since he's your husband?"

"I haven't said any vows, and you were there. My father put me in the bet. If you were me, wouldn't you want to know?"

Warner nods, thinking over my question. He gazes out again to the dining room, then back to me. "We all tried to tell Earl not to give out his livelihood over a full house. I wouldn't put it past a man like Weston to know how to play his cards right. What happened to Earl wasn't right, but what I do know is later, he came here. I think he was confused, thinking it was the boarding house. Sherman sent him out, and I heard he went to the saloon again."

"My father always did stupid things when he drank firewater."

"He was going on and on about all the money he had and how he would live high on the mountain like a king soon. No wonder with the railroad guy here. Only thing holding them up is a few claims of land they need and they're willing to do almost anything to get it."

I shake my head, cover my mouth to keep from screaming.

"I'm sorry. I wish I could help more. I can see throwing in the claim, but Weston goaded him, asking him if that was all he got. Buck mentioned you, and before we knew it, he tossed you in the pot."

"Figures," I mutter.

Warner glances behind him. "I best get going to check on the staff. You can tell Weston he can stay in room three tonight."

"Wait." I catch him as he goes. "He's not staying here?"

"A man can't run a business by giving out lodging on credit." Warner heads in the back and I tend to myself in the water closet. There's a damp dark mark down my bodice that will have to dry in time. It'll leave a watermark on the satin.

However, I doubt it's the first time a drink has been spilled on it.

Back in the dining room, our meal awaits. The gambler holds my chair out and when I'm seated; he startles me by pulling off my shawl. I go to reach for it, and he holds it behind his back. "It's far too hot by the fire, darling, for you to need this. Now what kind of husband would I be to allow you to become flushed and faint while trying to enjoy your company?"

I narrow my gaze, wondering what he's got up his sleeve this time. He sits across from me, the shawl on his lap. Picking up a fork, he cuts into his meat. His eyes sparkling, he takes a bite of his roast.

I run my tongue across my teeth, knowing full well he's enjoying the view.

"I hope you still have your appetite. It would be a shame to waste such a fine meal," he says after he swallows.

"Yes. It would." Not even the times I'd come into town with Pa did I ever get to dine as fine as this. To think I've been in the hotel dining room more in the past few days than I have in a lifetime.

I pick up my fork, placing my free hand across my bosom, and trying to ignore the fact my eyes are several inches above where his gaze is, and tell him.

The gambler gets up, coming over to my side. He takes my fork and picks up my knife, standing over me and cutting my food like I'm a small child. When he's done, he hands me back the fork, but then pushes my hair from my ear. "I adore your modesty, darlin'. As your future husband, I assure you, it is quite alright for you to use both hands. Unless, of course, you enjoy my assistance in feeding you."

My hand slides down a bit, my eyes going wide as I stare at him. The gambler once more sits on the other side of me.

"I'm not your wife."

"Yet," he says.

"How can you be so sure?"

He grins. "Because, darlin', if you don't meet me at the church by Tuesday, I'll see you in front of the Judge."

"And if I don't?"

His green eyes brighten. "Then I'll have no choice but to carry you through the streets of Deadwood kicking and screaming. The sheriff, the minister, and no law-abiding citizen will stop me as it's within my right." He pats his left side of his jacket.

My fist curls around the fork in my hand. He's wrong. There are at least one, if not two, people who'd stop him. Or would they?

A thought strikes me. I'm still one step ahead of the gambler. I relax my hold on my fork and twirl the prongs on the plate.

"Did you enjoy your chat with Mr. Warner?" The gambler sounds a little nervous, so I don't keep him in suspense.

"He said room three is open for you tonight, if you have the funds to pay. Oh, and my meal is free."

The gambler blanches, and I grin, taking a bite of my steak. I hope the bounty hunter is making out okay. Because right now, I think I got the better end of our deal.

14

The gambler's threat still lingers in the back of my mind. I'm running out of time. Tuesday will come before I know it, and I'm no closer to finding my father's killer and returning to the mountain than I was yesterday.

Warner's information might have given me a leg up on the gambler. He's a smooth one, my gambling man, but he's not as smart as he thinks.

It's cold in the morning. By the heaviness in the air, it's going to rain again soon. The May celebration is coming up, and here I thought we were still in April.

I spend the morning with Ruby, changing sheets and blistering my hands in scalding hot water to get them washed and ready to use again. We hang them on the back porch. My shoulders ache, but I'm grateful for a place to sleep at night that I can afford. First Grace at the dress shop, then Jensen at the Mercantile and Warner at the hotel. How many others in town does the gambler owe?

He's not much different from old Earl. By what Warner said, my father had to know about the railroad. How? We've been up in the mountains since the first snowfall.

They would have sent scouts ahead. Probably buying up or making offers as soon as they had their plans made to put down track.

It still made little sense, though. My father wouldn't have gambled it away, not that much of a sure thing. It made a girl think what was to become of her. If Earl would have sold the land to the railroad, Tail Feathers and his people would have been in danger. And what about me? Would he have still tried to marry me off?

I'd like to think not, but in my heart I know he would. Especially if he had other plans that didn't involve me. Plans with Amaryllis.

The rain comes. Fat. Heavy. Ugly. Ruby expected the stage-coach to come in by mid-afternoon. She suspects it holed up somewhere to wait out the storm.

The bounty hunter should have reached the claim by now, and I pray it all went smoothly. The last thing I need is for the bounty hunter to run into one of the warriors hunting or Chitto.

Something tells me the bounty hunter can hold his own.

It didn't stop me from worrying any less.

I change back into my pants, deciding I am better off without trying to wear a dress. There is no reason for me to go back to the hotel. I doubt Warner would tell me more.

Ella Mae mentioned Lincoln was out rounding up cattle and Buck would be with him. He'd be back in less than a week. Around the same time, the judge is due to come to Deadwood.

Had I met the gambler before my father bet me away, I might have seen the man differently. Maybe I would have dragged him to the church. He's attractive, But then again, would he be interested in me without my part of the claim?

On the other hand, the bounty hunter did funny things to the inside of me. Maybe because he has no interest in marrying me. Why is it a girl could become attracted to two men at once? I'm sure if I talked to Ella Mae's mother Pearl, she would tell me it was a sin, being the wife of a reverend. I think sometimes she sees me as one of hers, and it flatters me.

I used to dream my mother would come back for me. She never did.

I sigh. Rain or no rain, I put on my hat and first stop by the stables. One of my ponies is missing. Hank confirms the bounty hunter took it along with him.

I'm glad someone asked.

Also, I discover Hank rented my wagon out. I've been in town for almost a week. Since he didn't sell it, I'm good with him renting it out. It helps pay for the board of my ponies. I visit with Lulu. She's a pretty mare, mostly white with a splattering of black over her body. She has the palest blue eyes I've ever seen on a horse. Her knicker eases some of the strain in me from the last few days. I wrap my arms around her, inhaling the scents of horse, grain, and hay.

Hank tells me if I'm going to hang out for a while to make myself useful and clean my horse's stall. There's hay in the loft above, and I go up to get some for Lulu.

Up there, I can hear the steady pounding of the rain. It's cool and a few places on the roof leaks. Below, the barn doors slam shut, startling me.

I'm about to climb the ladder when I hear voices. I peer down, my heart speeding in the anticipation the bounty hunter has returned, but neither of the voices is his.

I hang back for a moment, squinting, then rub my eyes and look again. Putting down the hay, I move out of sight. What is the gambler doing here at the stables?

I suppose it would make sense he would have ridden a horse into town. I always kind of figured him for a stage riding kind of guy.

"I'd like to sell them," he says. "How much you think you can give me for the pair?"

I tilt my head.

"Not much."

"Then you can throw in the wagon, too. That will make them worth something, right?"

Hank's voice drifts away. It's too faint. I lean a little and hear the gambler exclaim, "What do you mean, the one is gone? Who took it?"

"Chord Townes," Hank says. "I suppose he'll be bringing it back when he returns."

"You rented him someone else's horse?" the gambler says.

I crawl to the other end of the loft where I can see and hear better. I crouch down, staying low and close to the wall.

The gambler looks around and frowns. "Well, when will he return?"

Hank shrugs.

"Well, when he does, the horse better be in good shape. I expect them to be sold. You can at least find a buyer for the other one in the meantime, can't you?"

Hank rubs his chin and glances down the row of horses and up a second in the ladder's direction. I breathe a sigh when he looks again at the gambler.

"They aren't your horses. Sorry, but there's a law about stealing horses and such. I don't get involved. If Jo wants to sell her horses, then she'll be the one to tell me."

I almost let go of the wall and stumble over the loft. I hold on and catch myself. The gambler thinks he can sell my horses!

I strut across the loft, heading for the ladder.

"As her husband, I have the legal right. I believe you're aware of the laws when it comes to women's rights and marriage."

I head down the ladder. How dare he!

"You aren't married. Come back when you are." Hank moves away. I hear the clanging of iron, and the gambler balls his hands into his fist. I jump down the rest of the way to the ground, catching his attention.

"Jolene." He takes me in. "What are you doing here, darlin'? Have you been up in the loft?"

My hat is hanging down my back. I take long strides up to him, my hand in a fist, my arm itching to pull back.

"What. Are. You. Doing?" My teeth clenched as I let the anger roll through me. Outside, thunder answers in response.

"I suppose you heard that?"

"How. Dare. You. Sell. My. Horses."

He holds up his hand. "Try. I tried to sell the horses. Surely, you understand." He spread his hands wide. "We can't tie them to the back of the stage, and I suppose we could ride them to Bisbee, but I was trying to think of your comfort, darlin'."

"I'm not your wife. Stop telling people I'm your wife!" I yell so loud it spooks several of the horses.

Hank keeps his back to us, lifting a horse's leg and settling the hoof on his thigh to shoe it.

"You are my wife. You *will be* my wife. Why are you being so stubborn? This paper here I've got where your father signed for you to marry me is as good as a contract or a marriage license. Any other woman would have swooned at getting a new dress, staying in a hotel, and traveling on the stagecoach and eventually the railroad. We can go east. New York. Boston."

I cross my arms and glare at him. The fist in my hand still tempted to connect with his jaw. "You said Bisbee."

"I've got business there, darlin', then we can go wherever you want."

"Because I'm the one paying for it. Isn't that right? You've been going around town, using up my credit at the mercantile and the dress from Grace's. Credit. You can't pay for the hotel room, and now you're trying to sell my horses."

Hank looks back, a nail in his mouth. He gives me a look, and I shake my head at him. He goes back to nailing the shoe on.

"My financials are none of your concern, darlin'."

"And why not? I'm your wife, remember?"

He scowls, those emerald eyes dark enough to cut through me as if they were diamonds. He's lucky all I got is my fist and not my gun.

"And as my wife, you need not worry your pretty little head over such matters. That's what having a husband is for."

I snort. I'm sure Hank snorts, or maybe it's the horse he's shoeing.

"And if I leave it to you, marry you, you'll sell my father's claim to the railroad and take the money and run."

"Jolene." He frowns. "Is that what you really think of me? No, my darling. The railroad is coming through. It's true the claim, my claim, *our* claim is worth a lot to them. They only need some of it. They're willing to negotiate, and you can still keep a piece. Think of it. Don't you want a nice house? A place to raise our family. We can start our own gambling hall right here in Deadwood if that makes you happy."

What happened to going out east? Or Bisbee. The man changes his tune a lot.

"No," I say.

Hank releases the horse's leg and straightens. He turns and watches us.

"No? I thought all you women wanted was a house and a man to settle down. Pretty dresses?"

"Does it look like I'm the dress wearing kind of girl?" I ask.

His gaze sweeps over me. "I can't help your father didn't raise you right. I hoped by introducing you to Daph—Miss Davenport—you'd become more comfortable in your woman ways. At the very least," his voice drops, and he takes a step towards me. "I have been looking forward to teaching you from a husband's perspective."

I clock him. My fist connects with his jaw, and pain explodes through my knuckles. I land the gambler flat on his backside. Standing over him, I shake out my fist.

"How's that for woman's ways?" I turn and look at Hank. "Thank you for not selling my ponies."

Adjusting my hat, I head back into the steady downpour of rain. The winds howl through the street, and few are out on a day like this. I don't blame them.

Perhaps, like the stage, the bounty hunter has holed up somewhere, too. At least if he is hunkering in a cave with our horses I won't have to worry about Chitto and him running into each other.

My hand hurts like I broke every bone inside it. Sucking in a breath, I try to keep the tears from rolling. Maybe I am not as tough as I thought. Maybe no one would want me for a wife except for the gambler after word got around.

I cradle my hand and walk in the direction of the doctor's place. A sign hangs on the door: "For emergencies, go to the barbershop." I moan at my own hot-headed stupidity.

By the time I get back to Ruby's, I am soaked to the bone. When I go inside, the house is quiet. Ruby likes to take a nap in the afternoons. She said it is her reprieve for getting up early then having to stay up late to see to her boarders. Right now, myself and the bounty hunter are the only ones here until the stage comes in again.

In the kitchen, I hear a sound. Stepping through the door frame, I find the bounty hunter, his jacket gone, his gun still strapped to his thigh. The darkness in the hall makes his hair darker, and his profile stretches between us as the light behind him casts a shadow on the floor.

"You're back," I say breathlessly.

He takes one look at my hand pressed against my heart and

frowns. I keep it pressed up against my chest to stop the throb-bing. My knuckles are turning from crimson red to deep purple.

"What happened?"

"I clocked the gambler."

His eyebrow shot up. The corner of his top lip lifts with it. Is that amusement or an involuntary reaction from the side of his face? I can't be sure.

"You punched Weston?"

I nod and wince as my mind replays the action and my hand throbs harder. I scrunch up my face, trying to keep the tears prickling in my eyes from falling.

"I thought I told you to stay out of trouble." He takes my hand in his. Tiny little zings, not at all unpleasant, crawl up my arm.

I'll blame it on the movement of my hand, but as soon as he places my hand in his to inspect it, the tears spring free.

15

"You know he's going to go straight to Sheriff Bentely."

He sits me in a chair in the corner of the kitchen. My throat burns as the tears won't stop falling. The bounty hunter takes a cloth and soaks it in water from the pump.

"He wouldn't."

The bounty hunter wrings the cloth out and crouches in front of me. He's so big, he doesn't go down much. "You've given him what he needs to push you to marry him."

He takes my hand again, wrapping it in the cool cloth. I wince and bite my lip.

"What happened?"

I take a deep breath to settle my nerves. The cool cloth helps a little, but mostly it aches more. "He got fresh with me." And I tell him about trying to sell my ponies. "Hank was there."

"Good." All this time, the bounty hunter stays crouched, his hands covering the cool cloth around my knuckles, the cords in his neck tense. He brushes his thumb over the top of the cloth. "I take it you haven't punched anyone before."

"I have." A long time ago when I was younger and the girls

in Chitto's tribe taunted me. I had always hung out with the boys, and I can see now how it would have made them jealous. I'd often get in spats and once, when two of them cornered me, I punched Running Fox in the gut. She doubled over, and her sister ran for their father. Earl had to appease the father by giving him the rabbits I caught that day for supper. He never would listen to me or take my side.

"Well, next time, fold your thumb in." He shows me and, through the tears, I smile. Those stone-cold eyes have taken on a different shade. They're unsettling. Not in a bad way. Concern etches over his face.

His thumb stops its caress, and all that's left on my face is the dampness on my cheeks. He leans toward me, and I hold my breath.

He gently pries my thumb from the clenched position on the cloth. "We'll wrap this against your hand. You'll have to let it heal."

"I broke it, didn't I?" It comes out hoarse, almost a whisper.

"I'm guessing so. Let's get this taken care of and we'll go see Bently before Weston tries to make a fuss."

When he moves away and goes down the hall, I breathe. Soon he returns with strips of cloth and Ruby by his side. They wrap my thumb and knuckles. "You won't be washing laundry for a few days," Ruby says.

"She can stay in my room," the bounty hunter says.

Ruby gives him a sharp look.

"Where are you going to stay?" My stomach does that flip thing and I try to tell it no. The thought of sharing a room with the bounty hunter sends my body into a tizzy and my mind in a frenzy.

"I got other places."

I guess there is the hotel, but it's more expensive. I can't let him give up his room. I shake my head, but the bounty hunter takes my face in his hands.

Ruby's eyes widen ever so slightly, but she doesn't say a word.

"You'll take the room. We'll square up on it later." I catch his meaning. He's referring to his percentage of my claim, although it makes my head go all fuzzy with his hands holding my face. "Don't argue."

He slips a finger over my mouth to keep it shut. "I'm tired, Dimples. Going up the mountain can tire a man out. You'll stay in the room, and you'll stay out of anymore trouble, you hear?"

I nod, and he releases me. "Good. Let's go see the sheriff."

Ruby watches as we leave. It's still raining, and I shiver. I never changed out of my damp clothes. The bounty hunter grabs his duster and instead of putting it on, he drapes it over my head to keep me dry as we cross the street to make it to the sheriff's office.

The gambler beat us there. The bounty hunter keeps a straight face, and I'm glad he's not the "I told you so" type.

"I'm telling you, Sheriff, I want to press charges."

Sheriff Bentely leans on his desk as we enter. "Against your wife?"

"She's not my wife," the gambler says.

"Finally," I say, and all heads turn my way.

"Yet," the gambler finishes, giving me a pointed look.

He's got a long red and purple bruise against his cheekbone and the side of his nose. I bloodied it, for his shirt beneath his embroidered vest has a sprinkling of brown from dried blood.

"I was defending myself." And I tell the sheriff about the gambler's plan to sell my ponies and how he got fresh with me.

Sheriff Bentely wipes his hand down over his face.

"Witnesses?"

"Hank," I tell him.

"You see it?" he asks the bounty hunter.

"No. I just got back in town after following a false lead." I wonder how long he'll sit in church on Sunday for stretching the truth.

"You bring back the pony you took?" the gambler asks.

"Nope."

"There. You see, Sheriff, he stole a horse and didn't bring it back."

I roll my eyes. "I gave him permission. He was delivering it to a family up in the mountain along with the supplies I promised them. Having to stay here, I couldn't let them go without necessities."

"I thought one outlaw from the Brownell gang was holed up at one of the abandoned claims. I told Miss Dean I'd deliver her goods on the way after she expressed her concern for the other mining families up there."

"And the pony?" the gambler pressed.

"I told him to leave it with one of the families. Their old nag had dropped during the winter and no sense in Kai getting fat in the stables. I only need one horse to ride home." I'd worry about my wagon situation later.

"Matter settled."

"But, Sheriff—" the gambler starts.

"Shouldn't you get back to the hotel? That jaw of yours has to hurt." The bounty hunter lays a hand on the butt of his gun as is his habit.

The gambler's eyes narrow. "Is that his jacket?"

"I didn't want the lady getting wet."

"Oh, she's no lady." The gambler storms in front of me. "But makes no difference to me, darlin'. I like a challenge."

I shiver uncontrollably as a droplet of rain from my hair makes its way down my spine.

The gambler goes to smile but his dimples never appear.

Guess that hurts. I cross my arms and watch as he goes to leave.

"Keep away from my future wife. Don't think I don't know about what happened to yours."

The bounty hunter stiffens. Sheriff Bently goes on alert. Both men have their hands at the ready of their guns.

Tugging on the lapels of his suit jacket, the gambler leaves. The bounty hunter leans toward the door, and I catch him with my good hand. Even the muscles in his arms are stiff.

"Pressure's getting to him. This whole town is getting out of hand. I could use a deputy for the weekend. Are you sticking around?"

"Nope." The bounty hunter plucks the leather duster off me, spins on his heel, and heads out.

I follow behind, my mind taking a minute as for the first time I use his name. "Chord… Um… Mr. Townes…"

He stops. The rain is dripping down off the porch roof above. "Don't go to the hotel tonight."

"I won't," I say to his retreating back without a chance to tell him about what Warner told me.

It doesn't seem as important anymore. I guess I'm not the only one harboring secrets.

I spend the rest of the evening at Ruby's. She brewed a pot of vegetable soup and biscuits. One of these days I'll ask her to teach me her secret to making them light and fluffy. Pearl taught me, but they're not nearly as good as Ruby's.

It's quiet between the two of us.

"You and Chord got something going on between you?" she asks.

"Why you say that?"

"He rarely gives up his room for anybody. Stays in the same room all the time."

"What if someone is staying there when he comes?" I ask.

"Oh, it's always there for him. I don't rent it out to anyone but him. He pays me by the month."

Interesting. The man is such a mystery to me. "You know him well?"

"Chord has been renting from me for years. Well, ever since he left the rangers and went solo." Abruptly, she gets up and starts clearing the dishes.

"Do you know why?" I shouldn't press, but I'm curious. One day it will get me in trouble.

"Not my story to tell." She gives me a sad expression.

"Does it have anything to do with him having a wife?"

Ruby sighs. "Had." She shakes her head. "You'll have to ask him."

Now there is a scary thought. I have never felt as if the bounty hunter would hurt me. Seeing the way he tensed in the sheriff's office makes me worry. What happened?

That evening, I stay in my room. Ruby says it doesn't matter as there is no one else there. I check for Shorty, keeping my hand just under the mattress and my other resting on my pillow above my head. It doesn't ache as much when I keep it above my heart.

I leave my boots by the door. They'll topple over if anyone opens it. I'm not afraid of Ruby. I've never feared staying here, but I have a bad feeling and it just won't go away.

Another day goes by, and my father's killer continues to walk free. As I lay in bed, I can't rest. If it wasn't Amaryllis, Warner, or Buck, it has to be the gambler. But he has what he wanted: the signed claim share and my father's signed note bartering me for marriage. There is no need to kill Earl. Did his temper flare with my father as it did me in the stables?

Then I remember, the gambler doesn't carry a gun. Or does he? He could hide it anywhere in that fancy suit he likes to wear.

Men!

When you think you've got them figured out, they throw you for a loop.

Closing my eyes, the bounty hunter's tense expression wavers in my dreams. Not tense, I realize, but sorrowful. The same kind of sorrow when Running Fox's husband got killed for crossing the border to hunt. He fought with the soldiers. Her anger and sorrow for losing one's love so early in life kept her invisibly chained inside the tribe's land after.

If the bounty hunter had once been a ranger, that means he is a man of the law. Something terrible must have happened for him to quit wearing the badge, but not enough to stop trying to bring criminals to justice.

It makes me wonder if he did have a wife. Where was she? Did she leave him? Or was she dead?

The sheriff is right. Things in Deadwood are getting out of hand. Worse, I fear I have run out of suspects. I have no other choice but to go back to the scene of the crime.

16

On Friday, I know I need to make it to the claims office first thing. Plenty of prospectors come into town looking to cash in their bits of gold. Any day now, many of the ranchers will return. I know this because every day this past week Ella Mae has pined for Lincoln, counting the days she hasn't seen him. The girl has it bad. He hasn't been gone nearly as long as she deems. I have a feeling the recent storm that blew through town and delayed the stage will do the same for the cowboys.

I really should have talked to Buck, and ever since I have this nagging feeling I need to see the fine writing for myself.

The claims office is a small building nestled beside the bank. It's run by a man named Jones. He doesn't have any other name, as his mother only knew his father as Jones. A last name, not a first, but it hasn't bothered him none. He's an older gent, with white showing in his beard. He keeps it neatly trimmed and his hair is dark like a raven's wing.

Jones stands at the counter, sweeping gold nuggets into a bag and putting them under his counter. Beneath, a latch clicks from the safe.

He pushes up a pair of wire glasses on his nose. "Whatcha got for me?"

I pull out the paper signed between me, the bounty hunter, and witnessed by the sheriff. "I need you to file this with the other paperwork on my claim."

"What claim would that be?"

I give him our land plot number.

He squints an eye at me. "And who be you?"

"I'm Jo Dean. My father is Earl Dean. That's our claim."

He gives me a good long look, then nods. "There's a Jo Dean on the land deed."

"That's me."

"Then you's got a problem, young lady. There has been a lot of action on that claim since Earl passed. Plenty of people trying to say they own it. Or at least his share of it. You're the second person today to come in."

The gambler won't give up. "Who else has been in here? What did they want?"

He shuffles to the wall in the back and pulls out a drawer of his filing cabinet. A grunt and huff later, he returns with our claim file.

"It's a mess. You're going to need the judge to sort this one out." He slaps the papers on the counter. I ignore the sound of the door opening to the right of me.

Jones spreads out the papers. "I'll be with you in a minute."

"I'm with the lady," the bounty hunter says and stands beside me. Suddenly, this side of the counter seems tiny. Picking up a paper, I read the promissory note my father signed over to Pierce Weston, a.k.a. the gambler. Then the bounty hunter reaches over me and picks up another piece of paper. It's a scribbled mess and the edge of the paper is ripped as if someone did it in a hurry.

The bounty hunter lays it beside the one from the gambler. It's between my father and... and Glen.

I take the paper from the bounty hunter's hand, careful our fingers don't touch. My other hand is still wrapped and my thumb, immobile. The swelling has gone down, but the memory of what caused it has yet to ease.

Earl used to complain if it wasn't one thing getting in his way, it was another. I can feel my father's frustration as I read it twice, each time feeling a little more nauseated.

"Do you know about this?" Jones asks.

"No."

"And there's this one." He Jones picks up another. The paper is worn and frail. Gently, I take it from him. The paper has been folded several times, the creases in a neat little square the size of a small photograph. I bring it closer to my nose. "Ew. Gross!" I take one whiff and drop it back on the counter.

The bounty hunter reaches over and picks it up.

"I know where this come from," I warn him. "You might not want to be touching that."

He puts it down. "Okay. Where did it come from?"

"My father's boot. The one that was missing. He had this folded up inside it. He did that. A lot."

"It was a woman who brought it in here." Jones taps a finger on the paper.

"Know her?" the bounty hunter asks.

Jones shakes his head. "Might have seen her at the saloon. Had a boy with her. Tall lad, maybe ten or twelve years old. I see him running around town more than I've seen the woman. She told him she couldn't trust him to deliver something so important."

"Amaryllis." It makes me wonder how much of her story she lied about for me to feel sorry for her. My father probably never left his boot in her room. She took it off his dead body. Before or after she shot him?

"It says here she's entitled to Earl's half of the claim if something happens to him." The bounty hunter slides it closer.

I'm careful not to touch it again. The entire thing is foul. "It's not legal, is it?"

Jones tugs at his beard. "Can't say so. Put it in the file for the judge to sort. She seemed adamant she got her share."

Why would Earl do that? What if he cared for Amaryllis like she said he did?

"You know about this?" the bounty hunter asks.

"No." Earl never meant to lose the claim in that poker game. He wanted to lose me. Without me, he and Amaryllis could be together without my interfering. The few memories I have of my mother were of her complaining about how kids got in the way of things.

"Amaryllis told me my father was special to her." I briefly recount my visit to her room.

"Lots of people want their hands on this land," Jones concludes.

The bounty hunter spreads out a few more pages. He picks up the deed—a copy, for the original is up in the mountains, unless Earl had it in his boot.

I freeze.

The bounty hunter must feel me tense beside him. "What?"

"What if someone has the original deed? Could they take our claim?"

Jones shuffles the papers more and pulls out another paper. "Says here the claim is a shared partnership between Earl Dean and one Jo Dean."

"That's me."

Jones grimaces. "I figured. You got something to add to this?"

The bounty hunter is busy reading the other documents. "Says here the railroad tried to make a claim on it saying Earl is dead and the land left unattended."

"Yep." Jones crossed his arm. "Which is why I voided it."

"With Earl gone, the land is mine," I declare.

The bounty hunter puts down the paper in his hand. "Except he signed off his portion to Weston. How long ago did this other claim against his half come in?"

"As soon as I opened my doors," Jones says.

"Glen," the bounty hunter and I say together.

"My father must have owed Glen on his tab."

"I took care of it when I got those supplies from him. Not enough there to warrant this. Even a judge will say it's so," the bounty hunter says.

Well, that brought a little relief.

"And the railroad?" I ask.

"They'll have to deal with you. The land still has ownership."

"Unless it's left unattended for too long," Jones points out.

A panic seizes me. "I need to get back up the mountain. What if they're already squatting at my place?"

"Calm down, Dimples. You'd have to be gone for a year before they could make the claim. You haven't even been gone a week."

"Like I told the fellow, Glen, when he came strutting in here, Mr. Weston still has a claim on Earl's portion. Can't both have the same piece of the parcel," Jones says.

"What did he say to that?" the bounty hunter asks.

Jones chuckles. "Got red in the face, said his claim was dated first. Told him the same as I told her." He looks pointedly at me. "The judge will be here Tuesday."

"That is, if the stage ever makes it on time," I mutter. Ruby waited for two days until she got a new boarder. A man came to answer a newspaper ad to help set up and run the new rail station. The tracks are not even in, and the railroad is trying to take over the town. They don't call this place Deadwood for nothing. Soon the railroad will get disappointed they chose this place. Or they'll have to rename the town if the train starts bringing in a bunch of new folks. As long as they stay off my claim on the mountain, I don't care.

"There's just a mark on this one, no signature," the bounty hunter says.

"Saw that, too." Jones taps on the paper. "Said Earl was too drunk, but he had a witness."

"And who'd that be?" I ask.

"Amaryllis."

"Of course." I take a deep breath and pull out the paper between the bounty hunter and me. "While we're at it, add this to the mess. I want it recorded proper so there is no misunderstanding like on my father's half."

Jones takes it, squinting at it. "They'll be pulling me in to speak to the judge about this."

"Good." The bounty hunter puts his arm around me. "It should have been taken care of days ago."

I catch the grit in his voice, the hardening look he gives me, but I don't back down. I could stand and stare into those cold, stone-gray eyes for eternity.

"You two going to get married?" Jones asks.

His question catches me off guard. Everyone assumes I'm hitched to the gambler. The bounty hunter stays stoic. He slips his arm around my waist. "I believe the lady is spoken for."

He steers me outside of the claims office. "I need some coffee." Withdrawing his arm, he heads toward the café. I feel a draft at my back, or maybe because his arm is missing.

"You coming, Dimples?"

As if I have a choice. Like a lost puppy, I'd follow him anywhere. Without the bounty hunter's help, I'll have no choice than to stand before the judge.

Inside the Deadwood Café, scents of coffee and sweet apple fill my nostrils. It's heavenly, really. All this time I've been in town, I haven't had to cook over a fire or fight with the potbelly stove in our cabin on the mountain.

My stomach grumbles a little, and I press my bad hand against it, trying to make it stop. The bounty hunter picks a table, and we sit near the window. The tablecloths are checkered in red and white, and none of the chairs match.

A woman swats away two children and picks up the coffee pot along with two mugs heading our way. She puts them down and pours without us asking. "I assume you want coffee," she says. "We have tea, but I don't take you for a tea drinking kind of man." She smiles at the bounty hunter. I can see the ring on her finger as plain as day. Then she looks at me and says, "Unless you want water."

"Coffee works fine," the bounty hunter says.

"You want some cream with that? We got some honey, and some sugar, too?" She flutters those lashes, and her voice gets husky.

"I'll take some cream."

"Oh, I'll remember that," she says.

"You?"

When the waitress's gaze goes to me, I realize he is asking me. "I'm good."

"You drink it black?" He doesn't seem to believe me.

"You got a problem with that?" I ask.

"Drink it how you like, Dimples." Then he looks at the waitress. "Is that apple pie I smell?"

"It is." The waitress's eyes light up with pride. "We've got cherry, too."

"Two slices of apple."

She goes off to fill his order. With her gone, I have a direct view of the ladies at the table near to us. Lottie Larson and Hannah Baker sit having tea and small sandwiches. Lottie's frown and Hannah's soft whispers make me uncomfortable. They're dressed in plain skirts with lace edged blouses. Lottie has her bonnet hanging down her back, and Hannah has hers on the table. At a table near the counter, two children sit, swinging their legs.

All I can think of is Jones's question. *You two going to get married?*

I hear Lottie laugh, give the bounty hunter a good sidelong glance. I keep my bandaged hand hidden under the table.

I sip my coffee. Its water compared to the kind I'm used to drinking.

"Problem?" the bounty hunter asks.

"What problem don't I have?"

"Not one that can't be solved. As I see it, you got to learn to read people. There are ones you stay away from and ones you tolerate. Very few do you ever trust."

By his expression, I can tell this isn't all about me. Deep in the depths of those cold stone eyes, there was once a man filled with warmth. Time hardens one's heart. Things happen, and it makes a person close themselves off from the world.

All I've known is that mountain up there. I'm not good at being social. I know how to interact with Tail Feather's tribe. Their ways aren't the ways of the townsfolk. They don't sit in a café to drink coffee, or sleep in hotels. They believe in a different God. Even though Ella Mae says it's a different version, we all believe in a higher being. Thanks to her and her mother, I know God is the first person to love me and the last to leave me.

Without Earl, I'm all alone.

It makes me wonder, what happened to the bounty hunter? Was he alone? Did he have anyone or any family out there to care about him?

"Is there anyone you trust?"

"Not anymore." He doesn't say another word as the waitress returns with two plates of pie. She sits one in front of each of us. I know I haven't got the money to pay for this. Already, I am indebted to the bounty hunter. I slide the plate toward him.

Maybe he intended to eat both. I'm not even mad he didn't ask me, not like the gambler when he tried to order for me at dinner.

"You can't tell me you're not hungry, and I saw the way you looked when we stepped inside. I could smell the apples baking. Go on and eat." He slides the plate back.

I bite my lip, trying to keep from turning red in the cheeks from embarrassment. There must be something in the air here to make my cheeks keep flaming as they do. I peek a look at Lottie and Hannah.

"Don't pay them any mind. You're here with me, and we need to figure out what to do with you while I track down this killer."

I snap my gaze back to him. He's serious. "What do you mean, what to do with me?"

"I can't have you in any more trouble." He takes a big bite out of his pie. As he chews, his gaze goes to mine. Darn him! I pick up my fork and take a chunk out of my slice. It tastes as good as it smells.

"You need to stay away from Weston. You don't go anywhere without me."

"What if I want to see Ella Mae?"

"Then she comes to the boarding house to see you."

"So, you're forcing me to stay shut in all the time?" I pause between bites. I've almost inhaled mine while the bounty hunter hasn't taken another bite.

"We've got three days until the judge comes. Weston isn't going to give up."

"The judge will just make me marry him, anyway." I slump a little in my chair. "Stupid Earl and his written promissory notes."

"Not if it's Judge Perry. Women run off and marry all the time without their father's permission."

I want to ask him how he knows, but think I better stick to worrying about my own matrimonial affairs.

"And if it's not?"

"The only other judge who comes around these parts is Orvis Stevens. He's traditional, and he sticks by the book."

"You know a lot about the judges. That because you were a ranger?"

The bounty hunter takes in a deep breath, his wide chest expanding.

"You're not anymore, are you? What happened?"

Okay, I shouldn't have said that.

The bounty hunter drains his coffee, reaches in his pocket, and throws some coins on the table. "Stay and finish your pie." He stalks out like a man on a mission.

I look down at the pie. Me and my stupid mouth. I twirl the fork and the waitress comes over. "Where is he going in a rush?"

"I don't know." I'm pretty sure it is something I said.

Lottie and Hannah rise from their table. Hannah ties her bonnet as Lottie patiently waits. I know they'd be able to hear me, so I say, "A man's stomach is a fickle thing."

The waitress puts her hand over her mouth and looks out the window, and I see Lottie and Hannah leaving.

"I'd best take this away." The waitress reaches for the bounty hunter's pie, one bite taken.

I put my fork in it, and she yanks her hand back. "His loss."

And I'm afraid it is.

And mine too.

A broken heart in my book is still a serious crime.

17

I spend the rest of the day with Ella Mae. She and her mother Pearl help me fix the blue dress from Amaryllis, and Pearl takes the pink dress as a personal mission to make it appropriate for a young woman like myself.

Most women my age are married and chasing after kids. Most because I know Ella Mae isn't, and she wants to something bad.

Reverend Carter is out making his rounds to see to the spiritual wellness of the community. During the week, the church is used for a school. He doesn't have much choice than to go out to the people. It leaves a quiet house for Ella Mae, Pearl, and her sisters.

I tell Ella Mae about what happened in the diner as we work on our mending. Twice, I jab my finger and give up. Ella Mae takes the dress and finishes putting in the new piece of lace Pearl found for it. The black lack is not a perfect match but it does its job.

I keep my hurt hand to my heart. Pearl gasps when she hears the story of how it happened. "Jolene Willow Dean," Pearl exclaims, "that's no way for a lady to behave." Then she surprises us and says, "A man like that deserves a good smack alongside the head."

"Mother!" Ella Mae exclaims.

"Sometimes a woman has to take matters into her own hands." Pearl shakes out the pink dress I brought back to her and eyes it wearily. "You'll find out soon enough there are other ways to keep a man in line."

Ella Mae's jaw drops a little. It makes me smile, and we all have a good laugh. While Pearl takes the dress to her room, saying she might have something to alter it, Ella Mae and I whisper for Pearl not to hear.

"And he left because you mentioned him being a ranger? Odd."

"I don't think so. Earl did the same when there was mention of my mother." Sometimes he disappeared for days. The first time, he left me for two days, and I found Chitto. He taught me to snare a rabbit and, after a while, showed me where his family lived hidden beyond Standing Rock in the mountain on our land.

"You'd best be careful around a man like Mr. Townes. He's an outlaw killer. He's nice enough when he comes for dinner, but my father says that it will take a lot of prayer to see the redemption for a man like him."

"What do you mean?"

"Lincoln says killing a man takes a piece of your soul. He figures Chord Townes doesn't have any soul left, which is why he can go around hunting criminals and bringing them back, dead or alive."

"But isn't killing a killer justice? They hang them after they have a trial." I touch my throat and wince.

"It's not our place to judge." Ella Mae puts a few more stitches in my dress and ties off the thread into a knot.

"Maybe this is his way of protecting innocent folks."

"Or maybe he's trying to ease his own guilt."

And I think of what Ruby said about the bounty hunter having a wife...*had* a wife.

No matter, I can't go getting all cow eyed and lovesick over a man like Ella Mae. She really loves Lincoln. Around here, people don't get so lucky for a love match. Why else would men have to put ads in the paper to find a bride? Perhaps I should put one in the paper for the gambler, then he'd leave me alone.

A feeling of unease seeps into my bones. I might have genuinely liked the gambler if not for his devious ways. And the bounty hunter... it's obvious he doesn't look at me as anything more than an extra ten percent income from my claim.

Men. Who needs them?

Ella Mae sure thinks she does. A part of me wouldn't have survived without Chitto. It seems one way or another they make you rely on them.

When Ella Mae's sisters are home after school, I take the blue dress and head back to Ruby's. Pearl invites me to stay for dinner, but I figure the bounty hunter might come checking on me. I hope he does because I want the chance to apologize. Ever since I ran into him on the horrid day of my father's murder, we've seemed to be nothing more than a pain in each other's side.

No, not a pain. I remember his hands on my face and the way he tended to my hand. Something is building inside me for him, and it's for the best to stop it now.

I said I wouldn't get in any more trouble but it's almost certain telling the bounty hunter I've got feelings for him would cause more than either of us could handle.

Back at the boarding house, Ruby catches me before I can go

up the stairs. "There's a Daphne Davenport here to see you. She's sitting in the parlor."

I duck around Ruby enough to peer inside, jerking back before Daphne can spot me. She's sitting in a wingback chair by the window. Her face lifts to the sun with her hands on her lap. She's wearing a bronze dress with a feathered hat.

"She's been here for over an hour. Insisted she stay until she spoke with you."

I press my lips to the side. The blue dress is in my arms, and I stare down at my boot-clad feet.

"I think I know why she's here. I need to take this upstairs to my room, and I'll be back down. Thank you for letting me know."

"Don't you go changing on her account." Ruby plants her hands on her hips. "Her fancy dress doesn't make her any more a lady than you. Pretty soon she and her father will ride the train right back to where they came from."

I smile, grateful for Ruby's support. I take a few steps on the stairs when Ruby halts me again.

"And that isn't all." Ruby lowers her voice, and wipes her hands in her apron. "I took on another boarder today. I told him he'd have to stay on the other end of the hall."

The way she says it makes my stomach flutter. Maybe the bounty hunter changed his mind and is staying at the boarding house.

Ruby's gaze flitters up the stairs. It's not the bounty hunter. My stomach sinks. "Who is it?"

She looks at me with a slight frown on her face. "Mr. Weston."

I almost miss the rest of her words for the loud pounding of my heart in my ears. "He is going to stay with us for the next few days."

Weston? Pierce Weston. The gambler. I glance over at the

parlor. So, that's why Daphne Davenport is here. She's come to see *him*.

But why does she want to see me? Unless he put her up to it.

"No sense in glowering," Ruby says. "I got tea brewing in the kitchen and dumplings in the making."

"But why?" I follow her into the kitchen, careful so Daphne doesn't spot me on my way.

"That's what I do. I run a boarding house and rent people a room to stay. I gave you a room." She picks up a wooden spoon and points it in my direction. Ruby's hair is twisted in a knot in the back. Her face is flushed from the oven.

"Did he pay you?"

She pulls back her shoulders. "It isn't any of your business, but yes. He did. In cash."

For Ruby's sake, I hope it isn't counterfeit.

I contemplate this recent change in events on the way to my room. I lay the dress over a chair and take a deep breath. For a moment, I close my eyes and envision being back in the mountains with the scent of pine and earth surrounding me.

Soon, I promise myself, feeling my freedom and hope slowly slipping from my grasp.

I head back downstairs to the parlor, deciding to get this over with fast. I try to ignore the fact the gambler is staying under the same roof.

Daphne stands as I enter. She smiles, her painted red lips set off from the rest of her powdered face. "Jolene. I hoped you would return soon. It's almost time for afternoon tea."

"It's Jo, as in Jo Dean," I say. "What do I owe this visit?"

"Well, Jodie, I wanted to invite you over to the hotel. We can have a late lunch and perhaps we can talk." The way she says my name sounds like Jo-Dee. As I go to correct her, I hear a wagon going down the street and the clip clop of hooves against the earth.

She asks again, "Lunch?"

"I've had lunch with Ella Mae. Thank you. Ruby's got tea here if you'd like."

"Oh, I'd hoped we'd do this at the hotel." Her painted lips turn down. She clasps her hands together. "Since I don't see the need for pleasantries, I suppose I should come right out and say it, shall I?"

"Let me guess. Since I'm a woman, your father sent you here to lure me into trying to get my land."

Daphne plops back down in the green cushioned chair behind her and laughs. It's a nervous laugh, or one of relief. "Oh, no." She waves her hand at me to sit opposite of her. "My father wouldn't hear of doing business with a woman or sending one to do it for him."

I frown, scooting over to the chair across from her. It's the one with the patchwork armrest. I'm not even offended by her father not doing business with a woman. It's the times, and like the expansion of the west, I figure one day things will turn and it'll be the woman running things. Probably not in my lifetime, so I lean forward with my elbows on my thighs, not at all lady-like and careful of my bad hand.

"Then why are you here?"

She straightens her spine and tips up her narrow chin. "Because of Weston, of course."

"Weston? I think you should go." I grab the chair arm with my good hand and go to get up.

Daphne puts out her hand to stop me. "You don' t even know what I'm going to say."

I stay seated, my fingers digging into the worn fabric of the chair. "He sent you to try to convince me to marry him. Well, you can tell him I'm not afraid of his threats."

"Good."

"Good?"

She nods. "I hoped to come here to offer my assistance."

"You didn't come to talk me into getting married?"

She shakes her head, leaning in closer. "On the contrary, I came to offer to help you escape back to that mountain of yours. Although I don't know why you'd want to go there and stay alone. Unless you're hiding something you don't want anyone to know about."

"Hiding something?" My blood freezes.

"Daddy says most folks bury their gold and money as they don't trust the banking system. I read a story back home about an outlaw who hid what he stole and won't tell a soul where it is."

"One can never be too safe," I mutter.

"I'm sure whatever you have hidden up there, my father would allow you to still access. He just wants the right of way through the mountain. He might even let you still pan for gold if you play your cards right." She wiggles her brows.

"Your father likes to play cards?" I ask.

"He, Mr. Conway, Mr. Warner, and Mr. Weston have had a game going on each evening after supper. I believe Mr. Weston made out well last evening. Daddy wasn't happy to part with half his purse."

Would the gambler pay up his debts, I wondered. Clearly, he hadn't won as much as Daphne let on since he moved in at the boarding house.

"Now listen up, Jodie, I have a plan," Daphne whispers. "They'll be taking another wagon of supplies to the rail workers in the morning. We could hide you in the wagon. If anyone finds you, they'll think you're a man dressed as you are."

Obviously, she must be blind not to notice the sisters are the size of twin mountains jutting from my chest.

"Anyway, once you reach the camp, you can slip off to your claim, grab the stash you're hiding, and Mr. Weston will have no choice but to move on."

I tilt my head, letting it sink in, as an understanding comes over me. "Mr. Weston still has claim to half my land."

She leans back and shrugs. "Daddy only needs the part where the mountain is."

"Is that right?" The entire lot is on the mountainside.

"You'd still have your part."

I hold off on asking who would decide which part was mine and which belonged to Weston. Or would that be the railroad after he sold it? And then where did that leave Tail Feathers and his people?

"I thought you didn't come here on your father's behalf about business."

"I see I'm going to be blunt about this. Mr. Weston is mine. I understand the circumstances in which the two of you got engaged. Clearly, the feelings are one sided and you don't deserve him."

I gulp like a fish out of water. "One sided?" I try not to choke.

She squirms in her chair. "That's right. Mr. Weston has feelings for you. It's not right to lead a man on. He even got in a fight over your honor and ended up with that nasty bruise on his face."

I covered my busted hand with my good one. Fight over my honor, indeed.

"If you have any consideration of anyone else's feelings, you'll get in that wagon tomorrow morning and stay clear of here. I'm sure once you're gone Pierce will get over you and he'll see what a fine woman I am, and we'll head on that riverboat he's always talking about."

I nod slowly, noticing how she slipped and used his first name. "Sure." I hear myself agreeing with her. "But there's one problem with your plan." Several if I pick it apart. "The sheriff said I can't leave town until the judge comes and my father's killer has been found to clear this mess all up."

"Daddy is friends with a lot of important people. Don't you worry about the judge."

The judge is the least of my problems. "And the wagon? Where will it be?"

"Behind the saloon. I heard Daddy say they were trading some crates of wine for some harder stuff."

"Shouldn't it have gone to the hotel?"

"Mr. Warner was shy on funds. So, you'll be gone? Tomorrow?"

A throat cleared from behind me, and Ruby stands with flour on her cheek. "Look out the window."

There, coming toward the boarding house, I spot the pinstripe suit. I get up and Daphne did the same.

I follow Ruby back to the kitchen. "Where are you going? Mr. Weston is coming," she says.

"Exactly," I say on my way out the back.

"Don't be gone too long. Supper is at six," Ruby calls. For a second, I feel the warmth spread in my chest. My birth mother never gave me a second mind as much as Ruby does.

I haven't gotten across the backyard where the chickens are penned up when I hear Daphne making a noise. She's got her skirts pulled up and is trying to tiptoe across the mud and straw.

I hold open the wooden gate and wait for her to cross.

"What are you doing?" I ask.

"It's rude to walk out on a person when we haven't finished our conversation. You are going to leave him, aren't you? He deserves a woman of refined quality."

"You should have stayed in the parlor for when he arrived. I'm sure it will devastate him to discover I'm not there."

"You're right." Daphne presses her hand to her chest, letting go of her skirt, to only yank it back up again.

She stumbles after me as I take the back path behind the buildings.

"Must we go this way? It's smelly and muddy and I'm going to get my skirt stained."

"There is a way between the buildings here. Be my guest." I sweep my hand out to indicate the path.

She wrinkles her nose. "You go first."

I huff, stomping my boots on the ground. I must have gone farther than I realize because as we come out between the buildings and step up onto the walk, I freeze.

Daphne holds her hand out. "Excuse me?"

I don't pay her any mind. She holds the side of the building. It's one step up on the plank walk. "Rude."

Not as rude as the scene before me. Standing outside the hotel are Mr. Davenport, Mr. Conway, and the bounty hunter. I know that leather duster anywhere.

I lengthen my stride, eating up the distance between us. Mr. Davenport and Mr. Conway both hold out their hands. "It's a pleasure doing business with you," Mr. Conway says.

The bounty hunter grips his hand first, then Davenport's.

Conway turns and goes back into the hotel. Davenport glances over at us. "Daphne, love, what are you doing? I thought you'd gone back upstairs to rest."

"That was hours ago, Daddy." She shoves past me. "I needed some fresh air."

"A woman shouldn't go about alone, especially in a place like this." Davenport holds out his arm for her.

"Jodie was with me." She says it again, pulling out the 'dee' and gives me a smug smile.

The bounty hunter rises a brow toward me. I shake my head.

"Your father is right. You shouldn't be out alone. There are some shady characters here in Deadwood." The bounty hunter locks those stone-cold eyes on me.

"You remember what we discussed." Daphne slips her hand around her father's arm.

I turn on my heel, deciding to go see Ella Mae again. Pearl's offer for supper is the escape I need. Before I can go far, the bounty hunter catches me by the arm. "Hold up there, Dimples."

I sigh, letting him come to stand in front of me. He keeps his hand on my arm, the one attached to my bad hand. His face is unreadable. Never a smile on his face and a tick in his jaw. "What do you think you're doing?"

I yank my arm from his hold, ross my arms, and wait as a gentleman tips his hat as he passes. The bounty hunter doesn't even move out of his way. The dusty cowboy looks like he came straight off the trail. There are several horses tied at the hitching post.

"Well?"

"I'm doing what *you* told me to do," I huff. "Or were you in such a hurry to get away from me, you forgot?"

The man is like a rock. No wonder his eyes are a cold shade of gray. His shoulders fall enough to take notice. He hooks his thumbs in his belt and I keep my eyes above his belt line. Anything else he's packing beneath is none of my business.

"Maybe we should talk off the street. Let me walk you back to the boarding house. Jo-Dee." He says it like Daphne.

"I can't help she doesn't know the difference between Jo Dean and Jodie."

"If you say so, Dimples."

He says it to send a thorn under my skin, but the way he says it is downright lethal. I don't seem to mind as much anymore.

"Fine, but just so you know, Weston has taken a room there."

The man would be unbeatable in poker. His face doesn't even twitch. He looks out over my shoulder a moment. A group of four men on horses come riding down the street from behind me. I haven't ever seen them before, but then again, I don't know most of the people who live in Deadwood. I guess that's what I get for living like a hermit with Earl in the mountains.

Two of the men have Calvary jackets on, but they're so muddy and torn I don't think they are in the Calvary anymore. I don't pay them any more attention.

The bounty hunter sure does. He keeps his gaze fixed on them as they ride by. He watches as they go further down and disappear.

I know better than to ask. He won't share with me none anyhow.

There is one thing for certain: Deadwood is about to get lively tonight. Question is, will it get rowdy enough to flush out my father's killer?

18

The new railroad station master, Ruby, the bounty hunter, and I enjoy a quiet supper of chicken and dumplings. It comes as no surprise for the gambler to not show up.

Ruby made an egg custard. She pours coffee, and we're entertained by Mr. Miles Clark. He's a good-looking fellow, been working for the railroad since he was sixteen. He's over twenty, keeps his hair combed to the left, and has the good sense to sit on the opposite side of the dining room table, away from the bounty hunter and beside Ruby.

"Has there been any more progress on tracking down Earl Dean's killer?" Ruby directs her question to the bounty hunter. She knows he and I are in cahoots. Why else would he stick around? For business, and nothing else, of course.

"There's a killer loose in Deadwood?" It's hard to refer to a man as mister when he's still wet behind the ears and fresh from the other side of the country. He's got one of those accents when he talks from across the ocean. Perhaps having him around will bring us a bit of luck. Besides, his voice is like a song you never want to stop hearing. You can't help relaxing while he talks. It's like a steady summer rain that both cools you and makes you feel refreshed.

"Someone shot my father."

"That's terrible. I'm sorry." Miles adds a little more sugar to his coffee. It wouldn't surprise me if the only thing they drink back east is tea.

I can feel the pressure on my chest. It's a hole in my heart I think will never heal, a sore spot I will have for the rest of my life. First, my mother abandons me when I was young. Earl gets shot and tries to marry me off. I got no family left.

Oh, if I don't start welling up to cry. I sniffle, take the napkin Ruby placed beside my plate, and dab at my eyes. *I will not cry over Earl.* Closing my eyes, a deep breath forces it back. The man tried to sell us out and trade me off. Anger, hot and steady, replaces the sorrow in a flash.

"I'm not." I stuff the napkin in my mouth. *Did I say that out loud?* By the expression on everyone's face, except the bounty hunter, I'd say I did.

"You have every right to be mad," Ruby tells me. "Jo's father made a deal before he died and it's caused Jo more grief than Earl's passing," she explains to Miles.

He eats it up like the egg custard. Hanging on every one of Ruby's words, he listens intently. How can a man seem so fascinated by someone's misfortune?

"Any suspects to who done it?" Miles finishes his coffee. Ruby makes a mean cup of black water that can bite back. Miles added enough sugar to sweeten a water trough. Lightweight.

"Sheriff Bentely is working on it. In a town like this, they could be long gone by now." The bounty hunter shed his duster when he came back to Ruby's place. He rolled up his sleeves, and the pale forearms don't match his tanned face.

"You get a lot of killing here?" Miles grips his cup.

"We get the usual." Ruby gives a warning look to the

bounty hunter. "They shoot it up at the saloon on Friday and Saturday nights, but our sheriff does his best to keep it contained."

"Lot more people coming with the railroad." Miles fiddles with the cup.

"Most won't stick around." The bounty hunter leans back. I'd almost think he was relaxed.

"Some of us can't leave." I cross my arms.

"Because of the killer?" Miles asks.

I nod.

"Not a soul you suspect?"

Ruby offers Miles more coffee, and he declines, awaiting an answer.

"Oh, I have a suspect." Then I shut my mouth. I shouldn't share anymore information with a stranger. Miles Clark wasn't even in the territory when my father was found dead. It wouldn't harm none to tell him. It's public knowledge. "You'll meet him soon enough. He's staying here, too."

"The gentleman in the room on the other side of mine?" Miles asks.

"He's no gentleman."

Slowly, Ruby gets up. "While that might be true, Jo, I know I taught you better than to accuse someone without evidence."

Ruby, too? He got to her in the matter of the time he rented a room. I hold up my healing hand. Money seems to sway even the best of people.

The bounty hunter remains stoic. He peers over at me, long and hard, as if he's drawing a picture of me in his mind. Maybe it's the curtains behind me. Ruby drew them closed as soon as the sun started setting. She's got two oil lamps burning at the table, and the soft glow against her skin highlights her age.

The bounty hunter and Miles talk more about the town

and suspects, and I notice any information not public knowledge is kept from Miles' ears.

When the meal is finished, Ruby gets up to clear the table. Miles offers to help her with the dishes. The bounty hunter gets up and slides on his duster.

"I take it you're leaving." I feel all domesticated standing up. While the bounty hunter may not be my partner in life, he's still my partner in tracking down my father's killer.

There is much we need to discuss.

I don't want to spook him again. I need his help to find this killer in the next three days. The pressure is on me, not him. His way of life doesn't swing in the balance.

I still need to know why he was with Davenport.

"I'm going to the saloon to see what I might find out. Weston will most likely spend his evening there, or at the hotel gambling."

"You know he's staying here. He'll come back."

For a man who never smiles, he's lips twitch and I swear they're about to crack, then they go straight again. "So will I."

The way he says it, the ideas it strikes in my mind will land me in jail. I'm almost certain they're against the law, but it's too late. My blood is heating.

He heads around the table. I take a moment to shove those thoughts into a jail cell of my mind and lock them away. For later.

A girl is allowed to dream.

I cut him off at the doorway. "We need to talk."

Yep, I sound like a nagging old wife. Earl used to tell me all the time how my mother nagged him about everything. The shack, the lack of gold, the cold, and sadly, me.

"Listen, about the café." He pauses a moment. "It's not wise to ask a man like me a lot of questions."

I asked one. Apparently, that was too many. "Why is that?"

"Because one day it could get you killed."

Killed. Is that what happened to his wife? Suddenly, my lips go dry.

"I don't mean any harm." I want to be his friend. Honestly, maybe I want more than friendship, but I'm willing to ride this out and see where it goes.

"Neither do I." I believe him. I shouldn't. Men like the bounty hunter are dangerous. They're killers for hire, this one preferring to stay on the good side of the law. I can feel it in my gut. The bounty hunter might not want anyone to know it, but he's good down to the core.

I've seen him at church, and a man who goes to church is one redemptive of his deeds.

Then he adds, "Don't think for a moment you'll get anything past me."

"Past you?"

"I know your secret, Dimples. I rode into that mountain. You said there were families in need of those supplies." He puts his hands on his gun belt. "Or should I say, rogue warriors? Families don't normally request tobacco and whiskey."

How did he find out?

"Medicinal purposes?"

Ruby doesn't allow guns in the house, which is why I keep Shorty hidden in the bed. The bounty hunter is different. Maybe because he was once a ranger. Maybe because he's here so much that Ruby trusts him. Or maybe because Ruby is afraid of asking him to lock it away in her safe, she allows him to keep it on him.

Either way, he's got me. A quiver starts in my chest and vibrates down my arms. I fist my hand and wince, holding it up.

The bounty hunter pulls his duster to smooth it over those broad shoulders.

"One warrior shadowed me up the mountain."

Chitto!

"I don't know what you're talking about." I decide to go the lying route. My stomach tightens and I tremble more. The egg custard might not taste as good coming up as it did down.

"Your secret is safe with me." He holds out his hand. "As long as you don't ask about my past."

By far, this is not a fair deal, but I take his hand and shake it, mindful to use my good one. "Deal." Those delightful zings race between my fingers. I almost don't want to let go and get the same feeling from him I can't risk anything happening to this hand until my other one heals. and pull it out of his grasp. We stand there. For how long, I don't know.

"The man who followed you. Is he okay?" An image of Chitto jumping the bounty hunter in the woods, or worse, the bounty hunter shooting him to cash in on his body to the government for him escaping makes me get a little lightheaded. My chest tightens.

"He took the pony and the supplies."

He's alive. Chitto is the last person up on that mountain I have left that I care about.

The bounty hunter clears his throat. "Stay in your room, Dimples. Unlock the window, but keep the door locked."

"Why would I do that?"

"You're asking questions."

I open my mouth to protest, but he says, "This way I can make sure nothing happens to you."

I scoff. It's not me he worries about. The man is trying to protect his investment. All I am is a share in a claim the railroad wants. For all the years I've been up there, there has been no great value or hope of finding a ton of gold or silver. We have been living off the land most of the time.

After he's gone, I help Ruby and Miles in the kitchen. Ruby tries to shoo us out of her way. Miles is insistent. I find it amusing the way he grabs a dish before she can wash it and

I've got the drying cloth. Ruby huffs. "Tenants do not wash dishes."

"Consider tonight your night off," I tell her.

"Enjoy some time to relax," Miles offers. "I promise I won't help you tomorrow." He winks at me.

"I'm not about to let the two of you alone in the kitchen," Ruby declares.

As we clean up, Ruby tells us where everything goes. We retire to the parlor. The two oil lanterns from the dining room follow us inside the room.

Miles and Ruby play a game of cards, and I politely excuse myself. Taking one of the oil lamps, I retreat to my room. Upstairs, I pause halfway down the hall. I glance over my shoulder behind me. I shouldn't, but I do. I go straight for the gambler's room.

I listen, straining to hear anything. Slowly, I open the door, surprised it's unlocked. Each room has its own key, and Ruby carries the master. I listen again, hurry inside, and shut the door. My heart hammering against my chest, I glance around the room. The drapes are pulled shut. The bed is neat, freshly made.

On the dresser, on the far wall, is a travel bag.

I bite my lip, freezing as the floorboard squeaks under my foot. I suck in a deep breath. Wait. I wonder if Ruby heard it downstairs.

All the boards creak in some place or another. Could she tell the difference if it reached her ears? I set the lamp on the dresser, not wasting any more time before I lose my nerve, and sort through the bag.

He's got a change of clothes. It's another suit, another vest, and between the vest and the shirt, I feel something soft and leather. I pull it out to find a small book. A journal of some type. I move to the light and flip it open. Names and dollar amounts glow in the lamplight. A few of the names have been scratched out and unreadable.

What kind of list is this?

Below I hear the door and swiftly put the journal back. Running my hands over the inside of the travel bag, I feel a lump. It's paper money folded into a pocket hidden by the lining seam. I don't count. I'm not a thief, so I return it to where it belongs.

I hear a voice with an accent and recognize it with a jolt. Miles will be heading to his room. I grab the lamp, head out the door, and race down the hall. When I reach the stairs about to go to my side of the hallway, I hear, "Is everything all right, Miss Dean?"

I glance back and smile, my stomach threatening to roll. "I was thinking."

"In the hall?" Miles asks.

"Don't you ever think of something that stops you in your tracks and you ponder it for a moment?"

"Aye. I suppose I do. Well, g'night."

I force my legs to slow down and walk normally. As soon as I reach the room the bounty hunter shared with me, I close the door and lock it. Taking a deep gulp of air, I head to the window and unlock it.

The night air sends a cold shock to my lungs. I gaze out the window and press my healing hand between the sisters.

Ruby's boarding house is one of the last houses on the edge of town. It's got a side yard and a backyard. And that's not all it's got. A large tree stands on this side of the house, close to the window.

I grin and lower the window back down. The bounty hunter is hiding more than he wants anyone to know.

I ready for bed, pulling on one of Ruby's extra nightgowns. I sit on the edge of the bed and watch the window. Shorty is still under the mattress on my pillow end.

This bed is bigger than the one in the other room. I could get lost in it alone. I try to stay awake as long as possible, curiosity getting the better of the fear trying to rear its ugly head.

I brush my hair twice and braid it seven ways to Sunday. This far down, the wind carries a faint hint of the noise from the establishments open after dark.

I've never stayed up and waited for a man to come crawling through my window. It almost makes me want to giggle. Butterflies hatch in my belly, tickling and feeding on this feeling. Not even Chitto has climbed a tree for me.

So, I blow out the lamp and wait. And wait. And the darkness mocks me. It mocks me until a chill sends me under the blankets. It mocks me until I can no longer keep my eyelids from dropping. It mocks me, for here I am, with my head getting caught in a dream cloud and my heart tied up in a deadly duel between feelings and facts.

I should have known the bounty hunter would learn the truth. It was worth the risk to get Tail Feathers his supplies to pay my father's debts.

Thinking of debts, I believe I owe Amaryllis a visit. She won't be able to talk her way out of this one.

19

It feels like forever for Sunday to come.

Every time I try to leave the house it is like Ruby can sense my intentions. It wouldn't surprise me if the bounty hunter put her up to it. I always wait for Ruby to knock and give me the okay to leave my room after the gambler vacates the house each day.

I half expect, half pray for Ella Mae to show up and give me an opening to escape. She never comes.

I leave the window unlocked. The bounty hunter is a tease. What's the sense of locking the door and leaving the window open if he isn't coming through it?

Ruby and I agree on one thing: there isn't any reason for us not to attend church this morning.

I'm in the middle of pulling on my boots when I hear a knock at the door. Thinking it's Ruby, I don't ask and open it. The gambler waves his hand and slumps against the doorjamb. "G'd morn, darlin'."

His eyes are glazed, his jacket a little rumpled, and his hair mussed. If I had to guess, I'd say he spent a night at the hotel playing cards, but I wouldn't bet on it. Not so much because it's

Sunday and Reverend Carter would say gambling is a sin, but more so because the gambler reeks of tobacco and something that makes my nose sting.

"I think you came knocking on the wrong door. Your room is down yonder."

"Oh, I know where I am," he says, those emerald eyes of his filled with intent.

"Be gone with you." I attempt to close the door.

"Am I interrupting something?" His head tilts forward, his gaze falling to the one boot on my foot, then tilts his head back to look over my face.

"Putting my boots on to go to church." My shoulders pull back. I don't have to explain nothing to him. He's not my husband.

There's a gleam in those emerald eyes which makes my knees feel a little weak.

"Looks like I came in time. Let me help you." The gambler grins and push against the door to open it wider.

"How about I meet you down at breakfast?" Where my stomach will unknot and Ruby is present to keep him from trying anything "fresh" with me again.

I try to close the door, but the gambler is one step ahead of me, or should I say, *boot*. He sticks his foot in the jamb and doesn't budge. "How about I come inside, and we get that boot on… or take the other one off."

I knew it. Sucking in a breath, I tuck my thumb under the way the bounty hunter told me. My fist curls behind the door. My thumb has been feeling better, but what else am I to do? Shorty is too far from reaching behind me, tucked in the bounty hunter's bed.

My lungs burn as I hold my breath and count. Slowly. One. Two.

Before I can get to three, I hear a booming voice call out, "That's not your room."

Relief floods me. I take a breath too deep, and gag a little over the ripe smell emanating from the gambler.

"It's not yours." The gambler wavers, holding onto the doorjamb as he turns to the bounty hunter. I never even heard him come up the stairs. My stomach knots up tighter.

"Actually," I hold up a finger, but the bounty hunter levels his gaze on me, and my finger goes down.

The gambler looks so smug, I almost feel bad for him. "Don't you have another outlaw to hunt?"

The bounty hunter pulls back his leather duster, reveals his gun, and the gambler snorts. "You may not have that here."

"Says who?" The bounty hunter looks past the gambler to me. "Finish getting ready there, Dimples. I'll walk you to church."

"Now hold on there a second," the gambler huffs. "If anyone is taking Jolene to church, it's me."

"I am not going to church with you." There is no way I'm going to play the part of the gambler's wife and lead everyone astray. Plus, he might try to waltz me up that aisle to stand before the good reverend.

An image of Daphne Davenport standing in my way almost feels like a challenge.

"I'm trying to be a gentleman about this, but you're making it hard."

"The lady lost her father. You should give her time to mourn." Sound advice coming from the bounty hunter.

"Even more reason for you to butt out."

Side by side, the bounty hunter has an inch, maybe two, on the gambler. They are about as different as night is to day. Both make my heart race in different ways. Both have features to make a girl swoon. Neither one is about to blink first as they stare each other down.

It's flattering. The gambler squints his eyes while the bounty hunter doesn't flinch.

"Okay, then." I step back, give the men their space and try once more to close the door but come up short. The gambler swings his arm out. His head turns. The expression he gives is dark and ugly for a moment. He blinks and puts his friendly demeanor back. Gives me a killer smile. It probably hooks most women. If not for the bounty hunter, I might fall hook, line, and sinker.

"Let her get her boots on," the bounty hunter says gruffly.

"Keep your eyes off the lady's boots."

Those are fighting words if I ever heard them. I am not sure what to do.

"You're in no condition to walk the lady to church."

"And you are?"

"I can walk myself." Ruby won't like it one bit if things get ugly in her hallway. I understand the gambler has a claim on me. But another part of me is fluttered over the bounty hunter sticking up for me.

Fluttered. Not flattered. I press my hand to my tickling tummy.

I know he's protecting his investment. That's all I am to him. And I keep reminding myself of it.

"You trying to stake a claim in my territory?" The gambler steps closer to me.

The bounty hunter shakes his head.

"Then back off." The gambler tries to shove his way into my room again while the bounty hunter grabs him by the arm and spins him around. The motion makes the gambler dizzy, and he latches onto the bounty hunter. "Take yourrr handssss offfff me!" the gambler slurs. "If anyone is taking her to the church, it's me. You hear? Me!" He points to his chest.

"Then you'd best get cleaned up. You don't want to stand before the reverend smelling like you've spent two days in a room full of sin."

The gambler lifts his jacket lapel, takes a sniff, and his eyes water. "You wait here, darlin'. I'll be right back."

The gambler staggers to his room. He shouts for me to stay. I hear the door open, then a great thud. The bounty hunter doesn't rush. I race past him, coming to an abrupt stop at the doorway. The gambler has his face planted in the fancy rug by his bed.

"You think he passed out?"

"Dead if he were smart."

Taken aback by the bounty hunter's remark, I crouch down and find a pulse. My stomach eases from the awful cramps threatening to seize. "He's still alive."

"Figured as much," the bounty hunter says from behind me. "Get your other boot, Dimples. Ruby's waiting downstairs. She doesn't like to be late for church, and neither do I."

I believe him. He's the type who would be on time for his own funeral.

Too soon. While my father's death lingers in the back of my mind, it's forefront on my heart. Crazy, mean old man!

His fault we are all trapped as we are.

It's the gambler's fault for doing whatever activities he's been engaging in for the past two nights. Ain't nobody going to keep me from getting out of this house today. Thanks to Mr. Clark and the note he delivered to Robbie, Amaryllis is expecting me.

"We can't leave him here like this. What if he gets sick and chokes on his own vomit?"

"He look like a baby to you?"

"No, but I saw it once. Everyone needs somebody at some time to take care of them." I bend down, reach across him, and try to flip him over. Another set of hands reaches between mine. Together, we pull the gambler over on his back. His head lolls to the side.

"Happy now?"

I glance over my shoulder. The bounty hunter is crouched, his face level with mine, ark brows furrowed together. His jaw flexes. I can't help looking at those lips held in a straight line. Suddenly nervous, I say, "Yes" a little too breathlessly. "Thank you."

He's up and back in the hallway in the blink of an eye. Holding out his hand, he says, "Come on, Dimples, unless you want someone else to find you in his room. Someone might find it inappropriate."

I catch his drift. Mr. Clark's room is across from him, I think. I haven't helped Ruby change sheets since the bounty hunter gave me his room. I don't know who is where except for the gambler.

Which reminds me, and as we return down the hall to fetch my boot and lock my door, I whisper, filling him in on my adventure in the gambler's room.

"You shouldn't have done that," he says.

I shrug.

"Tsk, you two," Ruby scolds, and we both look up from having our heads close together coming down the stairs. "Conspiring, and on a Sunday."

I'm right. Nothing gets past this woman.

"The gambler passed out in his room. We were concerned." I choose my words carefully.

Ruby pulls her shawl around her. "Serves a man right, being out for two nights and a day, playing cards no doubt and gambling away his last dime."

Except for the money he has hidden away. That, too, could be gone. "Poor man will have a headache when he wakes up again."

"Since when do you feel for him?" The bounty hunter holds the door open for us ladies.

"It's called being human." I say.

Ruby and I both take an offered arm and stroll down the street toward the church.

Deadwood is quiet. Eerily so.

I suppose it's what happens on a Sunday. The rest of the cowboys and the travelers are sleeping in from their two days of blowing off the dust from the trail. There are more people than last spring and the spring before.

It'll get even bigger with the train. With or without my land, the railroad will make it happen. Nothing stands in the way of progress. Chitto and his people are the first to attest to the cost of bringing the east to the west.

Throughout Reverend Carter's sermon, I sit along with Ruby and the bounty hunter. He takes a seat beside us in one of the middle pews. I'm surprised and tickled he would sit this close to me. Don't think for a moment I can't feel the furious stares of Lottie, Hannah, or Grace from two pews behind us.

Sorry. Not sorry, ladies.

Reverend Carter gives an enlightening sermon on fornication. By the eye rolls across the aisle, I'd say he's given this one more than once.

He's particularly wordy this morning. More than one of the town folks are squirming in their seats. Is it getting hot in here?

When Pearl rises with a book in hand, everyone else jumps to their feet. Reverend Carter no more than takes a deep breath when Pearl shouts out a page number. She belts out the first chord of a hymn, with everyone joining in. Reverend Carter raises his hand. He's about to shout another amen, when he slowly lowers his arms, takes one look at his wife, and joins in with song.

Beside me, the most startling voice sends shivers down my spine.

"You can sing?"

A deep rumble comes from the bounty hunter's chest. He

winks, and a chittering of giggles breaks out behind us. From this angle, it appears the bounty hunter may have winked at Lottie, Hannah, or Grace. A sting of jealousy ignites.

I press my lips together. As the song ends, folks make a dash to get out of the church. Lottie, Hannah, and Grace block the way. The bounty hunter does not know what he's got himself into, but I do. Standing on tiptoes, I can't see Ella Mae anywhere. All her sisters are up front and center with their mother.

"I'm going to say hello to Ella Mae." I scoot off before the bounty hunter can protest.

I search the front of the church. Pearl and the girls head out the side door, so I follow. Reverend Carter makes a mad dash to get to the front door to thank everyone for sitting through his lengthy sermon.

Still no Ella Mae.

Pearl appears annoyed, a slim line deepens between her brows. I don't have time to ask about Ella Mae.

"Jo. Wait." Robbie comes walking fast with a paper in his hand. He's got a tear in his shirt pocket, and it's pulled halfway out of his pants. A chunk of his hair is sticking at the side of his head and the dirt on his cheek.

Grinning, he holds out the paper. "I'm supposed to give this to you."

Before I can ask if he's alright, he takes off as a couple of boys go racing behind the church.

The bounty hunter hasn't left the building. Neither has Lottie, Hannah, or Grace.

I open the note.

Meet at the saloon. G.A.

I suppose Amaryllis could have another name. G.A. could also be Grace Adler. She wouldn't send me a note to meet her at the saloon, though. She would ask me herself. Nope. It's got to be Amaryllis. I best get going while I can.

Glancing over my shoulder at the church, my gut twists. Torn between going back in there and heading to see Amaryllis, the latter wins out. The bounty hunter is a big boy. He can make up his own mind. I'm sure the women have a lot to say to him about this morning's sermon.

I'll have to catch up with Ella Mae later, too. It's not like her to miss church.

The bounty hunter said I was to avoid the gambler. Since the gambler lies passed out in his room at Ruby's place, there shouldn't be any problem with me going to see Amaryllis.

Last time I spotted Ruby, she had taken up a conversation with a few older women.

This is my chance to slip away. Those women are going to hold the bounty hunter's attention as long as they can. Who am I to deny them his company?

I head off to find Amaryllis before I change my mind. No time to rescue the bounty hunter. I've got a killer to find.

20

The saloon is empty when I arrive. It's a little unnerving. I can almost hear the piano playing in my mind, hear the cowboys shouting and the women laughing.

There is a separate set of double doors on the other side of the swinging ones. They're unlocked and I go inside. The sun shines brightly outside. The air is warm and ripe with spring.

Here, however, the room is filled with gloom. Dark shadows and a haze left from all the smoking in this place linger. Closed, the place smells ten times worse than I remember. Chairs lie knocked over and one table is on its side.

Almost past the bar, I hear the clattering of glasses. "If it isn't Jo Dean," I hear my name and turn.

Glen hefts a crate of glasses on top of the bar. He leans forward and grins. Those beady eyes of his cause my flesh to prickle.

"Amaryllis is expecting me."

"Is she now?" Glen raps his knuckles on the bar. "Too bad she lit out of here yesterday."

Not believing a word, I place my hand on my hip. "When is she coming back?"

Robbie wouldn't have given me the note, and he wouldn't be here if she left, would he?

A fleeting thought sends my heart pumping. She's on to me.

Glen keeps those beady eyes fixed on me. "You okay? Let me get you a drink."

He grabs a bottle of whisky, pours a shot, and slides it my way. "On the house."

I put my hands up. "No, thank you."

"Go on," he insists. "It'll put color back in your cheeks."

I shake my head. "That stuff there is wicked evil."

He laughs, picks up the glass and downs it. His cheeks flare a little red, and he puts the empty down on the bar again. "Never took you for one of them tea sipping gals." He reaches under the bar, pulls out another bottle and holds it up. The amber liquid is darker than the last one. "Keep this one for the women." He licks his lips as he pours a fresh glass. "Looks like whiskey, tastes like iced tea."

"Any idea where Amaryllis went?"

"Drink. We'll talk."

Tastes like tea, uh? I need information. How much longer before the bounty hunter comes looking for me? Or will he?

I take the drink, knock it back. It's, as he says, iced tea, but more bitter than any I've ever had before. I wince and put it down. "Where did she go?"

"How am I supposed to know?"

"Did she pack up her things? Say anything? What about Robbie?"

Glen pours another round of drink for both of us. One for me out of the darker bottle and one for him out of the lighter one.

"Said she was about to come into some money. Too good to work in the likes of this place anymore." He lifts his glass, pauses, and looks down at mine.

Sighing, I pick it up. He waits until I swallow the over steeped liquid to drink his own.

"She say where this money was coming from?" With the judge coming in another day, counting on the stage coming on time, she must have believed her promissory note would land her part of my father's claim.

"Imagine she thinks she can claim a bit of the pot from old Earl. He made a lot of promises." Glen puts the bottles away. "That should do it."

His remark is odd. I tilt my head and the world tilts with it. I hold on to the bar and Glen comes around.

"I don't think that was all tea." My mouth feels dry, and I reach up to touch my lips.

Glen leans an elbow on the bar as he watches me. "I don't serve liquor to the ladies."

I blink. My mind is buzzing. He reaches for my arm. "I told old Earl not to make promises he couldn't keep."

"And what promises did he make you?" The heavier my body is feeling, the more it's coming into place. "Amaryllis didn't send me the note."

"Nah. That was all me, *darlin'*."

Only the gambler calls me by that, but I ignore him and ask, "You and Amaryllis?" I whisper. "You're in this together."

Glen snorts. "Earl said you were smart. Wild thing, he said. Likes to run around in those mountains." He's got his fat fingers around my arm. "He promised I could tame you once our deal was finished. All that firewater doesn't come cheap. Kind of suspicious, don't you think, needing that much liquor to hole up there in the mountains. Heard he took to stocking up on tobacco, too."

"That's why you had so much?"

"I knew Earl always asked for it when he came into town, twice a year. Knew Jensen stocked it for him, so I bought him out as much as I could. Your father had no choice than to barter with me."

"What did he barter?" I could hardly speak in more than a whisper.

Glen reaches with his other hand, slipping it around my waist. My hand lands on his wrist. I couldn't make it budge. He pulls me back against him. "You."

My throat burns, and my stomach cramps. I try to breathe through my nose and stay conscious.

"It was a good deal. I get you, and he got the tobacco and the liquor he was peddling up in the mountains. He owed me and promised me I'd get half the mine claim he had as your husband. We'd be partners. He got all the liquor he wanted, and we'd split the profits between the shipments up the mountain."

Taking deep breaths, I hate to break it to Glen. "No. Profit." The insides of my stomach boiling and gurgling. "No. Money. In. The. Trade."

Glen laughs. "You think I'm stupid? I knew the railroad was coming through here. We all knew from last summer it would reach us within a year or two. The land is where the money is, honey."

"My father didn't. Write. That note. Did he?"

"Your father tried to double cross me. Slapping down his share of the claim, I still would have had half. Then when he threw you in the pot, he went too far. He owed me!"

My legs are giving out. I try to pull away but can't seem to coordinate my limbs properly. "You killed him."

"He didn't give me a choice, but you do, sweetheart." Glen pulls me closer as my knees start to buckle. "Speak now, before the laudanum kicks in. When you wake up, you'll be Mrs. Glen Adams."

My stomach twists, and I struggle in his hold. "No!"

The door burst open. Robbie's eyes widen as big as an owl.

He stops in his tracks. My legs don't want to hold me up without Glen's help.

"Don't stand there, boy! I told you to fetch the preacher!" Glen barks.

"No! Robbie—"

Robbie looks between us. His eyes widen as big as saucers. Then he turns and runs.

"That's right, honey." Glen's grip is the only thing keeping me upright now. "The preacher will be here soon."

My vision blurs. The room spins. I can't feel my legs anymore. "You won't…get away…with this…"

"Who's going to stop me? You? By the time anyone figures out what happened, we'll be legally wed."

"No."

"Don't you worry. We can take a nice little nap in my bed until the preacher gets here."

Not going to let him get me in his bed. Not going to let the preacher think… I let all my body weight sag on Glen. He half-carries, half-drags me toward on the stairs. I reach for a chair, the table, anything to keep him from carrying me away. My fingers won't comply.

My stomach churns. I think I'm going to be sick.

Then, like an answer to a prayer I didn't know I was praying, the doors swing open again.

"Step away from her, Glen." The bounty hunter's voice cuts through my haze like a knife.

"This is a private matter, Townes," Glen says, but I hear the nervousness in his voice now. "The lady and I are about to be married. The preacher's on his way."

The bounty hunter's boots echo across the wooden floor. Through my blurred vision, I see him stop a few feet away, his hand near his gun.

"He…killed Earl." I manage to whisper.

"She's confused from wedding jitters," Glen says quickly.

"What she means is Earl gave me his permission to marry her. Women get too emotional at times, you know."

"What did you give her?" The bounty's hunter's voice goes cold as ice.

"Just tea. Ice tea to calm her nerves."

"Laudanum," I whisper.

"Let her go." The bounty hunter's jaw tightens.

"Now wait just a minute--." Glen starts to bluster.

The distinctive sound of a gun being drawn stops him cold.

Glen's face goes pale. His grip on my arm loosens and falls away. "It wasn't supposed to go like this. Earl double-crossed me! He owes me! We made a deal! The land is mine!"

The bounty hunter doesn't respond, just keeps his gun level and his eyes fixed on Glen. As if summoned, I hear more footsteps thundering outside. Sheriff Bentely bursts through the doors. Reverend Carter and Robbie are right behind him.

"What's going on here?" the sheriff demands.

"Confession to murder," the bounty hunter says. "Drugged her with laudanum. Needs a doctor."

"That's not—I didn't—" Glen sputters.

"Boy heard it," the bounty hunter nods at Robbie. "So did I."

"Me too!" I hold up a finger. My head lolls forward.

"Glen Adams, you're under arrest," Sheriff Bentely says.

Strong arms catch me before I hit the floor. The bounty hunter's face swims above mine for a moment.

"Stay with me, Dimples."

Then everything fades to black.

21

Something seems off. It takes a few blinks for my eyes to focus. I take a deep breath and stretch, my hands landing on a pillow. A patchwork blanket of blues and yellows is familiar. I know this blanket. I'm back in the bounty hunter's room. This is my bed because he let me use it.

I turn, reach under the mattress and my heart about stops. Shorty! Where is Shorty? Tossing blankets aside and up on my knees, I pull and tug. Where is it?

"Morning."

I pause. A husky male voice makes the blood in my veins warm. I know that voice as much as I know this bed.

Glancing over my shoulder, the bounty hunter drops his legs off the corner of the bed. One by one, then he sits up and leans his elbows on his thighs. "You looking for something?"

Twisting around, I land back on my butt. The bounty hunter hoods his eyes, and I wonder if he's fighting off sleep. Did he sleep here all night? I glance at the window, half open and letting a breeze in. I shiver and rub my arms. Somehow, I don't think the bounty hunter is tired anymore.

There is a breeze against the sisters. I clutch my shirt, but it's not my shirt. It's not the blue dress I had on either. Patting my chest, I gather the surrounding cloth. No wonder the bounty hunter is looking at me that way. First my derriere and now the sisters have both greeted him.

"My clothes?" I'm not sure I want to ask who stripped me of my dress and put me in this nightgown. It's Ruby's. I'm certain this is the one she lent me several nights ago.

He eases up out of the chair. "I had Ruby dispose of the dress."

"You what?"

"It was ruined," he says.

"How did I get here?"

"Don't worry, Dimples. The doc and Ruby took care of you."

"Glen?" He killed my father. "He was going to…"

The bounty hunter crosses his arms, standing at the end of the bed. "You're safe with me."

The tone of his voice causes me to relax.

I remember, he stopped Glen.

"How did you know where I was?"

"Robbie. He came looking for Reverend Carter. As soon as he said your name, I knew you were in trouble."

I wrap the quilt around me. "Thank you."

"What were you doing going off to the saloon on a Sunday?"

My fingers grip the blanket a little tighter. "I got to thinking about those promissory notes. One was for Amaryllis. She lied, or I thought she did. I figured she'd done it."

"And you went to confront her without me."

I shrug. "If I caught the killer then you'd be relieved of our deal."

"You still owe me, Dimples." He levels his stare with mine. Those stone-cold eyes have a darkening to them that can make a girl's insides get gooey.

"I aim to settle up."

"We'll worry about that later. You got bigger problems to deal with today."

"And what's that?" I gulp.

"The stage came in last night."

"No! It's early!" I'm up on my knees, both blankets clutched. "Was the judge on it?"

The bounty hunter's lips thin as he grimaces.

"We got a day, right?"

"Today's Tuesday."

Wait. I'd lost another day. I'd slept clear to Tuesday? "I should have known better to take that drink."

The bounty lifts a brow.

I wave my hand to dismiss him. "I've got to get dressed."

"Grace dropped off a new one for you a few hours ago."

I run my hand down over my face and try to shake the last of the sleep mites from my foggy brain. "Hours ago? What time is it?"

"It's near lunch. Ruby is in the kitchen preparing the noon meal." There is a twitch in his lips.

"What's so funny?" I demand, getting out of bed while keeping the quilt wrapped around me.

"You haven't asked about Weston."

"I'd prefer not to think about him. I suppose I'll see him soon enough."

He hooks his thumbs in his belt.

"Well, aren't you going to go so I can get dressed?"

He tilts his head. "The box is on the dresser; you can step behind the screen to change."

Squinting, I keep my eye on him. I inch closer to the dresser and pull the lid off the box. Inside is a gown as green as the mountain meadow.

"I appreciate her trading my dress, but I'd prefer my own clothes." I have had enough dress disasters to last me a lifetime.

"It's Judge Stevens," the bounty hunter says softly. "You'll want to wear a dress in his courtroom if you want him to listen to you."

I bite my lip, staring down at the dress.

"Go on, Dimples. It won't bite."

I pull the dress from the box. It's simple, with a floral print and buttons down the front. Beneath it are new undergarments, and... "What in the world?" I pick it up, trying to make heads or tails of the contraption. "I think this must have been put in here by mistake."

The bounty hunter covers his mouth for a moment, ducking slightly, and I dare him to laugh. I toss it to him.

His eyes go dark again. Those hooded lashes are dangerous to a woman's good sense. "This here, Dimples, is a corset."

"It's a what, now?" I don't think he said what I think he said.

"It's a corset. Surely, you've worn one before. I've seen you in a dress."

I shake my head when I should be nodding.

"It's an undergarment."

My hand slaps over my face. It's burning, no blazing red. "Put that down," I hiss. "You can't be touching that."

All I can see is his enormous hands covering where I'm guessing the sisters are supposed to be.

The bounty hunter laughs. He laughs! It's the best booming noise I've heard since he rescued me from Glen.

My heart thumps, thumping so much I don't know what's got me spooked more—the contraption or the man holding it.

"I'll step out while you put it on."

"Then what?" I eye him wearily.

"You put your dress on."

"I haven't ever needed one of those before." I point at it. By the way he looks at me, I digress. I grab the thing out of his hands and huff. "Then what?"

"We go see the judge and settle our business."

"Oh. Right."

After he steps out, I go about my business. I shed the night-gown and pull on the undergarments. Then it comes to the corset. The thing has more laces and ties than I have ever seen.

A knock comes at the door. "You doing okay there, Dimples?"

"I don't know how this thing works," I say through the door.

"Need some help?"

I look down at myself, standing there in nothing more than my chemise and drawers. It counts as being covered, right? Ruby would know how this thing goes on.

Never needing to ask for help much, I sigh. "Yes. I need help, else I won't be leaving this room."

My stomach grumbles in protest. I suppose it's lucky I threw up after drinking that nasty fake whiskey of Glen's. I might not have woken up, and then what would happen to Tail Feathers and his people? Chitto flitters through my mind. Who am I to think of protecting them when I couldn't even protect myself?

I wonder if Ruby found Shorty.

I don't have time to think about it more. The bounty hunter steps inside my room. My hands are across the sisters. "What are you doing?"

"You said you needed help."

"From Ruby!"

"Turn around, Dimples. No sense in taking Ruby from her kitchen."

This is a bad idea. A very bad idea. Those hooded eyes of his and the lift at the side of his lips send my nerves into a flurry.

"You know how?"

"Let's just say I know how to tie things up."

Hurriedly, I spin around before he sees the heat flare up my cheeks. I can't seem to control it around this man. My mind screams *this isn't proper.* Nothing about this day is starting off right.

Body heat wafts off the man, making me flush even more. He takes the ties and I feel the small tugs as he laces me up. Silly me, he had a wife once upon a time. He probably knows how to dress a woman and undress one. The latter part is what causes me the most distress. I shouldn't be thinking these thoughts. After Reverend Carter's sermon and Glen trying to get his way, I should know better.

The bounty hunter jerks on my laces, sending me almost back into him. He does it again and grunts for me to stand my ground. "You try to stand in place while someone is jerking on your laces," I protest.

"Grab hold of the bedpost."

I do as he says. "You make it any tighter and I won't be able to breathe," I whine. Sure enough, the corset constricts my ribs.

"That's the point." He yanks again, and I thrust forward toward the post, wrapping my arms around it. The bounty hunter flies forward with me, his chest colliding with my back. Sparks zing up my spine and I moan as he "oofs" at impact.

"Oh my." A crash sounds as I turn my head. Ruby stands in the doorway, a tray on the floor. A teacup spins, broken. Food splatters between the doorway and the hem of her dress.

"It's not what it looks like," I blurt, trying to push the bounty hunter away.

"Oh, it's what it looks like," the bounty hunter finishes tying my laces. "There, now go put your dress on so we can go see the judge."

"You're going to see the judge?" Ruby pats her chest. "Well, then. I suppose it should relieve me."

The bounty hunter walks over and talks to her in a low tone as he crouches to help her pick up the mess.

"Dress?" He doesn't look back, and I snatch up the dress and hurry to pull it over my head, the corset biting into my sides.

I smooth it out, then finish up the buttons in the front. The sisters sit comfortably in place.

Ruby places her hand on the bounty hunter. "Grace has an eye, doesn't she? Jo, that dress was made for you."

Deep down, I have a feeling it really was.

"I'll clean this up and you two come down to the kitchen. I've got leftover stew and fresh bread for lunch. I suppose you'll come back here after seeing the judge?" She looks at us both with an odd glint in her eye.

"One more night won't hurt."

The bounty hunter walks around me, reaches behind, and tugs on the back of my dress. "Sure."

My hands go back to cover my bottom. The bounty hunter raises his brow, and he's not wearing his long leather jacket. He's got a fresh shirt on, the color of the mountain sky. His hair hangs over his shoulders, and he holds his hand out for me.

He must have felt bad after I got drugged. Or maybe it's because he pulled these laces so tight I can hardly breathe.

"Wonderful," Ruby declares. "I'll bake a cake. Unless you want me to come down to the courthouse with you."

"That's kind of you," I say and stop. I hear a door close not far away. I'd forgot about the gambler. Almost.

Ruby scowls, glancing down the hall. She takes up the tray and heads for the stairs. The bounty hunter and me are not far behind her.

At the bottom of the stairs, the gambler steps out of the parlor, his arms wide and his grin even wider. "Jolene. Darlin'! You're up and about! Thank goodness."

"Is that a new suit?" I shouldn't have asked. He tugs on those lapels and opens his jacket to reveal a red brocade vest with gold threads. He is wearing a black tie around his neck and his hair is combed neatly in place. More impressive are those emerald eyes that make a girl feel like she's the prize. He sets them on me. "Don't worry about the dress. We can have an entire wardrobe made in the latest fashion. Right now, am I ever glad you're okay. With all this nonsense of your father's killer out of the way, the judge awaits us."

The gambler offers his arm and says to the bounty hunter, "I'm grateful for you seeing her safely returned to me."

I do a double take. Maybe he hit his head on that floor a little too hard.

Ruby clucks and says, "I think I'll come after all."

The bounty hunter transfers my hand to the gambler's arm. "I'll be right behind you."

Somehow, it doesn't make me feel any better.

I might have caught the killer, but it's time to face the law.

22

The Deadwood Courthouse is in the schoolhouse. Yep, it's the same building where children learn and we all go on Sundays to hear about God. While the children spend the day outside and take a field trip to Johnson's café, court is in session. Doesn't seem the right place to pass down judgment on criminals, but law in Deadwood is a relatively new concept.

Judge Orvis Stevens is a bald man with a mustache and jowls like a hound dog. He sits at the teacher's desk off to the left of the pulpit. We all sit and wait our turn in the pews, the bounty hunter on one side of me, the gambler on the other. Ruby sits in the pew behind me. The railroad men have come to witness the outcome. Mr. Davenport and Mr. Conway give a nod our way.

There is a woman in black wearing a veil to cover her face. My heart goes out to her. It's bad enough to become a widow, then to have to stand before the judge.

"Jo Dean," the judge calls.

I don't like the way he says my name. All three of us stand. The gambler gets out of the way as I walk past him. The bounty hunter isn't far behind me.

"Here." I say, determined not to let my knees knock.

"Interesting." Judge Stevens runs a thumb down the side of his moustache as he absorbs the fact I'm a woman. By the way he looks at me, I'd say he's not impressed. The bounty hunter may have been wrong to put me in this dress.

"You Pierce Weston?" Judge Stevens asks.

"That would be me, Your Honor." The gambler raises his hand and comes to stand on one side of me. A dark gash swipes underneath his one eye. It's an ugly dark mark put there by my fist. He sports it without so much as a wince in my direction. "I appreciate you coming all this way to finally put all this nonsense to an end."

"Don't thank me yet." Judge Steven glances around, his neck never moving. "Chord Townes?"

"Judge Stevens." The bounty hunter steps on the other side of me.

"Never thought I'd see you in my courtroom again."

"Same."

There is no time to dwell on the fact the judge and the bounty hunter know each other. It's part of the past, the one I agreed not to question.

"Wait a minute," the gambler says. "What's he have to do with this?"

Judge Stevens holds up his hand. His black robe sleeve slides down his arm. "I'll ask the questions here."

The gambler crosses his arms.

I hold my hands in front of me, twisting and interlocking my fingers.

"Let me get this straight," Judge Steven says. He's got a stack of papers in front of him. I recognize them from the claims office.

Behind us, the door shuts, and we look back. Amaryllis and Buck slip into the last pew. She's got a lot of nerve showing up here, and with Buck. What's he doing here?

Over my dead body will anyone get their hands on my claim. I ball my hands into fist and curl them into my skirt.

The bounty hunter looks over at me, gives his head a shake, but I can't relax. The more the judge shuffles through the papers, the more tense I feel.

"Miss Dean, you and your father own a claim on the mountain."

"Yes, sir."

"Your father is deceased."

"Yes."

"Seems a lot of people have a claim on your father's share of the land."

"Now, your honor, if I could add, not only is the land claim due to me, but Miss Dean's hand in marriage is mine as well. You can take care of that while we're here, can't you? With her status, surely, you can see that would entitle me to act on both of our behalf."

"Status?" I burst out.

He glances down at my fist and steps a little further away. My hand aches a little as I try to keep from clenching it.

The bounty hunter leans in and whispers, "Calm down, Dimples. Let Judge Stevens handle this."

Easy for him to say. It's not his land, honor, or life on the line here.

"Your Honor?" Ruby stands, waving her hand.

Judge Stevens leans to look around us. His eyes shine with a bit of interest. Well, wouldn't you know? "And you are?"

"Ruby Hazelton. I own the boarding house here in town."

"You have something to say that pertains to this case? Fact. Not hearsay," Judge Steven says.

"Fact." Ruby lifts her chin. "Jolene can't marry Mr. Weston. This morning I found her and Chord, I mean Mr. Townes in a... a..." Ruby fans her face as she says, "compromising situation."

Judge Steven peers over at the bounty hunter. "Is that right?"

My jaw falls to the floor. I'm busy trying to pick it up when the gambler gives the bounty hunter a deadly look.

"He was in her room while she was ill. We all were checking on her, or trying to." The gambler turns his glare toward Ruby. "Nothing *compromising* about that."

"Jo slept in Mr. Townes' bed, and he stayed the night. I know what I saw this morning when I brought them breakfast." Ruby grips the pew in front of her.

"She's lying, your Honor. My room is right down the hall from the one where she is staying. I never saw Mr. Townes go inside."

"You came through the window," I say, turning to the accused.

The bounty hunter doesn't flinch. His voice never wavers, and he looks straight at the judge when he says, "That's right."

"Did you or did you not spend the night in Miss Dean's room?" Judge Stevens' eyebrows raise.

Ruby raises her hand.

Judge Stevens nods at Ruby.

"Technically, Your Honor, the room is Chord's. I mean, Mr. Townes. Miss Dean has been sleeping in his bed for several nights now."

The gambler tenses. He growls over at the bounty hunter. Any moment I suspect he'll pull something deadly from his sleeve.

I reach over and smack the bounty hunter in the arm. "What are you doing?"

All I want to do is sink into the floorboards and disappear. Everyone in the room stares at me.

Those stone-cold gray eyes meet mine. "Trust me, Dimples. You'll thank me later."

"I object!" the gambler declares.

"You would!" Ruby puts her hands on her hips.

"Now ma'am, I'll be the one to handle this, don't you worry." Judge Stevens winks at Ruby. I try to close my eyes and wash the sight from my mind.

"It's all lies, your Honor. The two of them are in on this scam together. Don't you see? He's trying to take the land for himself," the gambler says. "It's all part of their plan."

"And what plan is that?" I ask.

"The plan to take all the money for yourselves," the gambler says.

"Money?" Judge Stevens tilts his head. "Ah, yes. The railroad. Well, this matter isn't over money, so your accusations have no merit in my court, Mr. Weston. Now, as far as the matter of marriage, Mr. Townes, you're prepared to take Miss Dean as your wife?"

My blood goes cold. I stare at the bounty hunter, my vision blurring.

"I am." He looks straight at the judge.

"With all witnesses present," he motions to Ruby, then to us. "I hereby declare you, Mr. And Mrs. Townes." Judge Stevens smacks his gavel.

Like that?

"Now wait a minute!" the gambler objects.

"What?" I look at Ruby as she picks up her bonnet, grinning from ear to ear. I can hardly breathe. It wasn't supposed to happen like this. Ella Mae always talks about church weddings and the part where your man kisses you to seal the deal.

The bounty hunter isn't puckering, he's grimacing. I'm certain he flinched when the gavel came down.

Can a judge do that?

I suppose they can. They are the ones who decide on the law here in the territory. Whatever happened to asking a girl first?

The gambler shouts in a fury and the judge smacks his gavel again. "Enough," Judge Stevens roars.

"You might have got the girl, Townes, but the land is still mine!" the gambler says.

My lungs hurt with the effort to breathe. This cursed contraption around my ribs is going to be the death of me. Someone should have told Glen corsets, not drugs, were the way to take a woman down.

Hot, angry tears sting my eyes and run down my cheeks.

"Jo?" the bounty hunter says.

I pinch my nose and close my eyes tight to shut off the waterworks.

"On the matter of the land," I hear Judge Steven say, "since the deed is half in Miss Dean, excuse me," he says, "Mrs. Townes' name and her late father, Earl Dean, Mrs. Townes maintains her half of the land under the supervision of her husband as by law."

My eyes pop open.

"And the other half?" the gambler demands.

I put up my finger, when from behind us a woman shouts, "Your Honor? Oh, Your Honor!"

We all turn. The woman in black comes forward, tripping over her skirts, and trying to pull up her veil. "If anyone is getting that half, it's me!"

She huffs, flinging back the long netting of her black veil. She swishes it aside like a horse's tail trying to ward off a fly.

Judge Stevens puts down his gavel. "Who are you?"

She pulls out her handkerchief from her sleeve. Dabbing her eyes as she sniffles. "Polly Dean, Your Honor. Earl Dean was my husband."

The bounty hunter's hands come up to grip my arms. "Steady."

I feel lightheaded. "Mother."

"That's right, Honey Buns, Momma's come back. That

nasty man is gone, and now we can have everything we've ever deserved."

She's serious. The woman has eyes full of horse manure and lips as red as a viper. Crow's feet jut from the corner of those eyes, neither damp nor sorrow filled.

She opens her arms, trying to pull me in, and I step back into the chest of the bounty hunter. He wraps his arm around my waist and Polly takes the hint. She covers her mouth and nose with the handkerchief, sniffling. I'm sure it is a fake sob. "I've imagined this day for years."

"Yeah, I bet you have," I mutter.

I feel the bounty hunter's chest rumble against me.

"Mrs. Dean," Judge Stevens says.

The gambler shakes with a violent tremble. He paces in front of the pulpit and back again. "Surely, your Honor, the promissory notes are legal?"

"They're legal," Judge Stevens says.

I suck in my breath.

"Anyone else want to put in a claim while we are at it?" Judge Steven spreads his arms, looking at everyone in the pews.

"I do!" Amaryllis's voice rings out. She stands up when Buck grabs her by the shoulder and pulls her back down. "He promised me!"

Then Buck says something into her ear, and she sits her butt back down, crossing her arms.

"None here, isn't that right, Amaryllis?" Buck says.

She scowls and says, "Fine. No claim here."

Polly's shoulders sag, and she appears relieved. I think I'm going to be sick again. It's probably best I skipped eating before we came to see the judge.

"In that case, I grant Mr. Weston half ownership of the claim formally known as the Dean property."

The gambler grabs those lapels and nods. "Thank you, Your Honor."

Polly screams "No! I'm his widow, it's my inheritance!"

"Don't thank me yet," Judge Stevens holds his gavel mid-pause. "Having had an extra day to review this case and, seeing how a new situation has come up," He points at the bounty hunter and me. "I first assumed this was a closed case of marrying the daughter to the new landowner for a full claim of the land. Seeing how you are now half owner, Mr. Weston, and Mr. and Mrs. Townes are half owners, it seems only fair to declare half the value of the land be paid…"

Polly bounces up and down. "Me!"

Judge Stevens growls and she goes quiet.

"Mr. Weston, you will hold ownership of fifty percent of the land, unless, of course, Mr. And Mrs. Townes come up with the market value of the land in which they have one month from today to pay. I will hold any funds earned from the land in escrow until the month is over and we settle the land ownership."

"When you say one month is that thirty days or thirty-one?" the gambler asks.

"Thirty-one."

"What about me?" Polly struts right up to the judge. "What do I get?"

Judge Stevens lands his gavel. "My condolences on your loss, Mrs. Dean."

Polly says a few choice words and struts right back the way she came. She pushes between us and glares at all three of us. "This isn't over yet."

"Your Honor, let's be reasonable," the gambler protests.

"Thirty-two."

"Wait a minute. You can't do that!" the gambler exclaims.

"Thirty-three," Judge Stevens says.

"What am I to do with only half?"

"Nothing," I chime in. "You won't have it for long."

"Dimples," the bounty hunter warns.

"Next case." Judge Stevens tries to shoo us away.

Mr. Davenport and Mr. Conway stand. The gambler shoots daggers at the bounty hunter with his eyes. "This isn't over, Townes." His expression softens. He turns those emerald eyes on me. "*Jolene.*"

He heads toward Mr. Conway and Mr. Davenport. An exchange of glances goes between the bounty hunter and the railroad men. I never found out what they were talking about. I guess there is a lot I'm going to have to learn, secrets included.

"You're pale. Let's get you back to Ruby's and get some food in you."

Ruby offered to bake a cake.

"Did we just get married?" My head is still spinning.

The bounty hunter takes me by the chin. I blink to clear my vision. Looking into his eyes, searching for a sign, any kind of emotion, I fall short. His lips flutter up. I hold my breath. My eyelids flutter.

"Don't worry, we'll keep it in name only, Dimples."

"Anyone else got something they need to settle? I don't have all day!" Judge Steven declares.

The side door bursts open, and in comes Lincoln with his hands raised high over his head. Behind him, Ella Mae points a sawed-off shotgun in the middle of his back.

The bounty hunter and I spring apart.

"Ella Mae!" I exclaim.

"She's crazy," Lincoln says. "You need to get the sheriff."

"What's the meaning of this?" Judge Stevens stands.

"This man took advantage of me, judge. I demand you marry us." Ella Mae's hair is all askew. It's like a wild goose made a nest on her head. Lincoln's shirt isn't tucked the entire way.

"Son? This true?" Judge Stevens asks.

"She kissed me first." Lincoln shrugs. "What was I supposed to do?"

I roll my eyes and stop. I know that sawed-off shotgun. "Shorty!" I stalk up to Ella Mae and grab my shotgun from her.

Ella Mae tries to hold on to it. "I need it. I'll give it back when I'm done and married."

"What are you doing?"

"Ask him!" she exclaims.

"What have you done?" I lower my voice.

"He's been visiting the Swanson sisters. I did what any sensible woman would do in my situation. Don't you dare let him get away!"

I snatch Shorty.

Lincoln lowers his hands and goes to take off when the bounty hunter grabs him by the shoulder and I turn Shorty in Lincoln's direction. His hands fly back up.

"Now ladies," he says. "This is a big misunderstanding. Ella Mae, you don't want to get married this way. We should do it in a church."

"We are in the church." Ella Mae juts out a hip and puts her hand on it.

"She's got you there," the bounty hunter says.

"Man up, son," Judge Steven says.

Ella Mae grabs him by the arm and yanks him in front of the judge. "Jo, you're my witness," she says, trying to fix her hair with one hand.

As I stand there, watching Ella Mae and Lincoln tie the knot in front of the judge, I can't help feeling I'm the one who got cheated. I thought finding my father's killer would bring resolution and freedom.

Ella Mae pulls Lincoln in for a kiss, keeping a hold around his neck much longer than any man can go without air. If their kiss is any sign, I'd say their marriage is going to be a lot more than in name only.

WHAT'S NEXT?

Give a girl a husband, a debt, and a bounty to collect... and she'll turn the town upside down.

The bounty hunter wants to keep our marriage in name only. The gambler isn't above blackmail, and the whole town is in a tizzy over the railroad coming to Deadwood.

Over my dead body!

Okay, maybe not mine, but when the new railroad owner is accused of murder and puts out a reward to catch the actual killer, what's a girl to do?

My claim is at stake. Maybe my heart, too.

The sooner I return to my home in the mountains, the less heartache I'll have. No one catches the bounty hunter, but the gambler is on to us. The bounty hunter has been side-stepping me ever since the judge declared us husband and wife. If I can't rope him into a proper marriage, the gambler will take more than my precious land. All he must do is prove to the judge the bounty hunter and I haven't sealed the deal. His attempts to woo me are getting hard to resist.

I'm desperate enough to hunt down this bounty on my own.

And given the circumstances, I can't afford not to get my man. Getting the reward money will pay off my debts, but it may also become one big disaster.

Get your copy of **THE COWGIRL TAKES THE BOUNTY** *so that you can keep reading today!*

ALSO BY SUSAN LOWER

Silver Wind Equine Rescue Series

Love horses, cowboys, and second chances? The Silver Wind Horse Rescue series has both! While the members of the Silver Wind Horse Rescue set out to provide refuge for abused and abandoned horses, those very horses may be the salvation they need to find a second chance at love.

Forgotten Reins

Unbridled

Silver Stirrups

Hearts of Hidden Hills

Sweet and wholesome small town love stories filled with second chances and healing families provide a wonderful, feel-good read.

Residence of Her Heart

Salvaged Hearts

Reckless Hearts

Brides of Annie's Creek

Travel back to the old west where these women take love into their own hands and learn somethings can't be rushed.

Fruit Cake Bride

Thimble Bride

Postage Stamp Bride

ABOUT THE AUTHOR

Growing up on a farm in Pennsylvania, Susan Lower yearned for adventure. A woodsy gal, Susan prefers camping over going to the beach any day. Still a farm girl at heart, Susan writes fast action reads filled with cowboys, heroes, and hope. She writes both western historical and contemporary romances, romantic suspense, and has been itching to one day write a mystery or thriller. Christmas is her favorite holiday, and she loves to write resilient characters struggling to overcome the complications of life while holding their values and strengthening their faith.

www.ingramcontent.com/pod-product-compliance
Lightning Source LLC
Chambersburg PA
CBHW020619180626
46810CB00007B/2847